Liberating Rhonda

Beau Johnson

Dedication

I want to thank my Editor, Karin, for her creative ideas and skillful organizational contributions while she was working with a rookie writer. Without Michael Ray King's writing course, Go Write and You Won't Go Wrong, to help me organize my thoughts into chapters I would probably still be wandering around the literary badlands. I also think of Michael Ray King as my writing mentor, and truly appreciate his guidance and support at every step in this project.

Chapter One

"No way! I just gave her a few compliments. How can those hurt her feelings? That's crazy! I've gotten lots of compliments in the past, and not once were my feelings hurt. Not once!"

Marc was fuming. He could not understand what this girl's problem was. *Why on earth is she upset?* To his way of thinking, when guys and girls get together and are getting along pretty good, maybe even dating, he'll give her compliments and she'll give him compliments. No big deal.

"When one of her friends asks about me, I'm sure she tells them good things. And when some of my friends ask about her, I tell the truth and say really nice things about her, too. What's wrong with that? Compliments are a good thing, right? How can she possibly take it wrong? I like compliments! Doesn't everybody?"

Marc had given Rhonda some compliments while they had been "dating," but she had given him many more. Not all were meant or intended to be shared with what ended up being a handful or so baseball buddies at their high school. But Marc didn't really give much thought to the possible consequences on her.

"She can tell all her friends all the good things about me she wants to—I like it!"

Rhonda was trembling and unable to speak when she first met Marc in 1968. Their romance was a very physical one, and he would always leave their passionate meetings in the forest and at her house pleasantly relaxed and calm. Each time those visits were concluded, Rhonda was absolutely thrilled and would excitedly relate each and every detail of their romance to her best and most trusted girlfriend, Gwen.

Marc told his best buddy, Robby, and eventually a handful of his horny baseball buddies about Rhonda's romantic assets, including her warm, soft, and very kissable mouth and her natural sexiness. Soon, a half dozen or more athletes knew a lot about her, too. She gained quite an exciting reputation among those guys.

Marc gained something of a reputation among the girls, too. "I *betrayed* her? Bull! I only said nice things. Very nice things. *Incredibly* nice things! All the girls think I'm some kind of monster just because I told some of my buddies how great she was? That's fucking nuts!"

Rhonda Bell had lived next door to Gwen O'Rourke since first grade, and over time throughout their elementary, junior high, and high school years they became BFFs (Best Friends Forever).

The two girls spent literally hundreds of hours at each other's houses. They jumped rope, played jacks, tag, house, tea party, hide-and-go-seek, dodge ball, marbles, Red Rover, and cowboys and Indians in their yards with the kids in the neighborhood, and they had least a hundred sleepovers at one house or the other. Each girl had a sister two years her junior.

Their parents became good friends and neighbors through the years, and the two families frequently celebrated birthdays and holidays together. Both mothers liked the other woman's daughters and over time came to the conclusion they were nice girls and good influences on each other. Gwen was more serious and studious, as was her little sister, Alice. Rhonda, on the other hand, was outgoing, fun-loving, spontaneous, adventuresome, and social, very much like her dad, Wesley.

Mr. Bell worked as a mechanical engineer for a growing national company and traveled all over the six surrounding Midwestern states at least four or five days a month, building the business in his region. Feeling guilty about being gone so much, to compensate for his work absences, he took his family on frequent vacations to fun places, usually in the summer, when the kids were out of school. Fishing, sky diving, motorcycles, and camping out were his favorite hobbies and he often worked them into the family outings, one way or another. He taught the girls to swim when they were four and six, and to snorkel in the Bahamas two years later. Scuba lessons were promised when they got old enough. Because Rhonda related so well to her father's fearless attitude toward life she became something of a "daddy's girl."

Rhonda's mom, Teresa, a former kindergarten teacher, was much more protective than, and not nearly as daring as, her husband. She often feared for her daughters' safety during many of the family trips her husband planned, such as camping in the Rocky Mountains or hiking along the Appalachian Trail.

Teresa much preferred they take their vacations in places like New Orleans for the French Quarter and Canal Street, Atlanta to explore Underground Atlanta, and Miami to immerse themselves in the Latin cuisine and culture. She also enjoyed the more mundane yet fun, and less risky trips to the beach. Teresa tolerated local fishing excursions too, even though her husband would often spring one on her and the girls at the last minute: "Let's go fishing at the lake tomorrow, okay? Who's in?"

Wesley taught his daughters and his wife to fish from the shore in a local freshwater lake, Lake Lilly, and bait their own hooks, in spite of Teresa's barely-concealed distaste for slippery worms and slimy fish.

Even after the girls learned to swim, Teresa would not allow them to fish from a boat on the lake. In her eyes, danger lurked everywhere, and Wesley, all in fun, of course, would taunt and tease her sometimes just to see her freak out:

"I'm going skydiving tomorrow. Who wants to go with me?"

*Wes can kill himself diving out of perfectly good planes if he wants, he's a grown man, but my girls will **not** be going with him—ever! He'd also better be fully insured!*

Teresa had to put her foot down, at that point.

I like the fact that Wes is honest, hard-working, and not afraid of many things, but these are girls! If we had boys it might be different, but we didn't. These are my girls!

When Rhonda turned ten Teresa reluctantly allowed her to take short, slow rides around the block on the back of her husband's Honda motorcycle. His eldest daughter loved hugging him tight around the waist in the warm sun on those brief, intentionally slow trips, feeling very close to him, and very excited to be on a real motorcycle.

"Slowly…Wes…she's only ten, remember? S-l-o-w-l-y."

When Rhonda hit twelve, however, Teresa put a stop to the motorcycle rides. "You are a young lady now and it doesn't look very ladylike to be riding on the back of hot, smelly, loud, dangerous machines!"

Mostly, she didn't want Rhonda to take a liking to motorcycles and the bikers who rode them.

4

When Rhonda was being bullied in the fourth grade by Berta the Bully, a bigger girl, her dad enrolled her in judo classes *and* took three years of classes with her.

"She cuts in front of me in the lunch line and shoves me when we are playing outside! I tell her to stop but she just laughs."

Berta backed off some months later when she saw Rhonda wrestling with one of the smaller guys, Lenny, before gymnastics class. Standing up, fingers head-high and entwined like on TV, moving right and left in a semi-circle, Rhonda wound up throwing him hard to the mats with a full-body hip throw, landing Lenny flat on his back and knocking the wind out of him.

Knowing Berta was watching Rhonda glared at her afterward, the message clear: *I can do the same thing to you, bitch!*

But when Rhonda sprained her ankle in a tournament, it was just the excuse Teresa was looking for to put a stop to any more judo training for her eldest daughter.

"That's it! No more judo for you, Rhonda. I *knew* you would get hurt, and you did. Enough rough-housing! It's time to learn to be a young lady. You can take ballet with Patricia if you want."

Even so, the five firsts, three seconds, and a third place out of the eighteen judo tournaments Rhonda had entered for girls in her age group and experience level bolstered her confidence considerably.

Rhonda's little sister, Patricia, was a much more serious student—straight As, Honor Roll, and inherently studious—and hung out with Alice, Gwen's little sister, most of the time. Like

Gwen and Alice, Patricia took ballet instead of judo, much to Teresa's relief.

The older girls shared few common interests with their little sisters and spent little time with them. The developmental two-year-plus physical gaps were significant.

Gwen and Rhonda enjoyed growing up as neighbors and were always together. They shared hundreds of major and minor secrets during those early years and grew quite close and trusting of each other even before adolescence arrived.

When puberty finally arrived, they painted each other's nails, washed each other's hair, and even showered together. They leafed through fashion magazines to see the latest trends, debated about cute guys, color coordination, skin care and makeup, movie stars and their relationships, music, cool kids and cool clothes, Mean Girls and bullies, and who liked who. They discussed hair care, cuts and color, hormonal problems, parent conflicts, and profanity, and gossiped for hours at a time.

Gwen was almost eight months younger chronologically than Rhonda and looked her age, but she was just as curious and hormonal about boys, sex, romance, and the intersection of all of those three main teen interests.

"You won't believe what just happened, Gwen! It happened! Come over quick!" Rhonda whispered furtively into the phone one afternoon.

Experiencing her first period six months before Gwen at age thirteen, it initiated hours of excited discussion.

With the hormones of puberty came shared fantasies about which boys at school were cute, lusting after them privately, which pop teen idols and rock stars were the best and the cutest, also lusting after them, and often discussing for hours all of the anatomical and hormonal changes they themselves were going through.

Their sleepovers and discussions were a rehearsal for dating guys. The girls didn't know it then, but puberty was preparing them for adult romantic and sexual relationships, and eventual childbearing and raising families of their own.

Monthly school dances began, bringing with them excitement and anticipation. "What if a guy asks us to dance, Gwen? We'll be so embarrassed. We don't know how to dance!"

So the girls taught themselves to dance together, slow and fast, watching themselves in the full-length mirror on the back of their closet doors in their bedrooms until they didn't look so awkward, clumsy, and uncoordinated, just in case some boy asked them to dance.

They also learned how to kiss by practicing on each other, just in case some boy wanted to kiss them sometime.

A girl in their class, Eva, had played spin-the-bottle at a party with three guys there. Because she puckered up in the back room just before being kissed, one of the boys later made fun of her to the other guys, saying she looked like a fish feeding. Her nickname after that party became "Fish Lips."

Boys can be so cruel.

Eva was mortified, humiliated.

Gwen and Rhonda were going to make sure *that* was *not* going to happen to them. "Where do your hands go when kissing, and how do you know which side to tilt your head on so you don't bump noses?" Rhonda asked with a giggle soon after word of Eva's horrible experience got around.

"Do you press your lips firmly or softly? Lips open? What about tongue?"

"At what point do you close your eyes?" Gwen wanted to know. "Do you always close your eyes? Do you hold your breath? Breathe through your nose? How long should a kiss last?"

Their questions were plentiful, and they were answered by trial-and-error and practice.

They carefully watched how couples kissed in movies and on TV to see how they did it and rehearsed often at night during their sleepovers.

Eva did the same with her best girlfriend, Sissy, and never received any criticism for her smooching skills or technique again.

A little awkward and weird at first, the more they practiced kissing the better they got at it and the more fun and exciting it became. Gwen and Rhonda truly liked and cared about each other and were such close friends that it turned into a more normal expression of their mutual natural warmth and affection.

"Kissing is *so* nice! You're my favorite smooching partner, Gwen, but don't tell anyone." Rhonda's confession was followed by many giggles, laughs, grins, and groans.

French kissing became an important step in their romantic educational process and where they learned about the passion associated with kissing.

"I admit kissing is great fun, but French kissing you is even better. I could kiss you for hours! It makes me feel so warm inside … and excited," Gwen admitted with some embarrassment.

Slowly but surely, step by step, kissing on the mouth led to kisses on the face, the eyes, the nose, then the ear, a tongue in the ear, and sensual and strategic kisses on the neck and the shoulders.

"Oh, baby! When you kiss me *right there* on my neck it sends shivers right thru me. I love it! Try kissing my shoulders gently, too. Mmm, yeah! Right… *there*."

"It tickles when you put your tongue in my ear, but it feels *so good*. Let me put my tongue in your ear to see if you like it… Do you like this, too? What about…here? Okay...my turn…"

Giggles led to groans—and a temporary pulling away and halt when things started to feel *too* good. Then, after a lot of smiles and laughter, eventually they would start up again, but then evolve into a little more conservative sensual exploration.

It was not unusual for one or the other to spend several hours or more exploring any one area, drift off to sleep for a while, and pick up where they left off upon awakening, sliding back off to sleep again ten minutes later.

During months of weekend sleepovers, the girls slowly explored each and every sensitive inch of their respective faces, lips, and necks, taking turns, giggling and laughing, then moaning. Hands roamed free above the waist for a long time, too, and then legs and thighs were explored in a gradual process of light and long strokes and caresses, all the way south to the toes.

At this stage, manual bush exploration was off limits by unspoken, mutual agreement. However, intertwined legs moving up and down together with the one on top, usually Rhonda, sliding her thighs in the moist, warm crevice between Gwen's legs, evolved into one or occasionally more of their usual grunting, groaning, amazingly satisfying finales. But they never really admitted it or talked about these mutual orgasms. It was just one of the private benefits of sleeping together, it seemed to them.

Even after they had become fairly confident kissers, which was the original goal, it didn't stop the sensual sleepovers, smooching, hugs, tentative touching, and sharing.

Practice makes perfect.

Chapter Two

Twelve was when Marc's curiosity about girls and sex really began. But because his dad was very traditional and conservative, and very inhibited and uncomfortable talking about sex, Marc didn't get his birds-and-bees talk until he was fifteen, a haltingly awkward sixty-second conversation while briefly fishing together along a canal bank. Their talk mainly consisted of Marc's dad asking him if he knew how to "protect himself with girls."

Nodding affirmatively, Marc guessed his dad was talking about rubbers, a subject about which he had a lot of questions and few answers.

Getting his son's quick nod, his dad abruptly declared their fleeting fishing trip and father-son talk to be over, so they packed up and left, never to broach a sexual topic again.

If Marc's mom hadn't insisted his father take him fishing and have this abbreviated talk with him, it wouldn't have happened at all. The parental obligation had been fulfilled, but not much inter-generational knowledge or guidance was passed on.

As a result, Marc was never prepared like Rhonda, Gwen, and most girls his age who had reached puberty, not even close. He got most of his information about topics like sexual relations, birth control, and sexually transmitted diseases from older boys in the locker room or from the pages of pornographic magazines. Of course, these sources were rarely realistic and almost never reliable.

Anthony, one of Marc's buddies since first grade, was the one to explain the anatomical intertwining and positioning of sex to Marc when Anthony was in the sixth grade and his buddy was in the fifth. The basics of what goes where and how were explained in a matter of ten minutes.

In addition he even claimed to have been having sex with willing girls since the fifth grade, but Marc didn't believe him, at first.

The girls Anthony is talking about appear like such nice girls, and they're only twelve! They barely have any visible boobs!

No, Marc decided he flat out didn't believe him.

Anthony was four inches taller than any of the other guys and could punch like a mule. He was easily the toughest sixth-grader in their elementary school. One day, in the hall he introduced Marc to one of those girls he claimed had been having sex with him, Marsha, who just giggled, and blushed, although not denying it in the least. Anthony assured Marc that since she was a sixth-grader Marsha would never think of screwing him because he was only a fifth-grader. *I guess she only likes tough guys who are at least in the sixth grade.* The girl had her standards.

At the end of the eighth grade, Anthony also claimed he had been screwing Linda Rosen at her house a couple nights a week over the past year while her parents were at a movie or out to dinner. She would open the back door to her bedroom and let him in, literally and figuratively, Anthony said, but it didn't become general knowledge until the week before he moved away.

Marc found it hard to believe him, once again, and decided he was just bragging.

To prove his claims, Anthony took Marc and Robby with him when he made his last visit to Linda's house, at nine-thirty at night. Her parents were at a movie that night, and she was supposed to be doing homework. Instead, Linda was apparently doing Anthony.

Marc and Robby were hoping to become Anthony's regular replacement studs with Linda, individually or together. All they were looking for was a blowjob from her, or to play with her titties, at the start. *Robby and I are hoping Anthony's endorsement and introduction will do the trick.*

The two guys waited for forty-five minutes in the dark alley behind her house until Anthony finally returned. Exiting very quietly thru the back door from her bedroom, his shadow made no noise as he moved towards them. A broad smile on his face, he appeared very relaxed in the darkness.

"I told her I'm moving next week and offered to introduce you guys to her, but she passed. You guys are only seventh-graders. Maybe if you were in eighth grade…who knows?"

Linda would choose her fuck buddies, supposedly, and seventh graders were not on her list.

Only tough eighth graders will do.

Finally it sunk in to Marc that some girls his age were probably having sex, in some form, and he was being left out. Anthony hadn't provided many details and hadn't mentioned anything about him bringing a rubber to Linda's house.

After he had gone, Marc asked Robby, "Do you think Anthony is screwing her without a rubber?"

"I don't know. A used rubber would have been a little weird, but it would have been proof that he'd screwed her."

"Naked pictures of Linda would have been pretty convincing," Marc added, "but nobody I know has access to a camera or a darkroom, and I doubt she would let anybody take naked pictures of her anyway... It was a great thought, though, Robby, as she apparently does have a nice body."

So they had to take Anthony's word.

Of course, Marc didn't think Linda or Marsha was having actual sex, either. *Maybe she had just given Anthony a head job. Even that possibility is pretty cool because it means Linda and/or Marsha is sexually available to the right guy.*

"I'm a little annoyed Anthony hasn't passed on more about his supposed sexual adventures before, if they even really happened, Robby," getting a nod in agreement.

"Now Anthony is moving away, and he has not told me or any other buddies any real details about his sexual experiences, even though we have gone camping three or four times together in the nearby woods with him and some of our other buddies. Has he said anything to you Robby? He should have said something. That's what good buddies do."

"Nope, he didn't say anything to me, Marc!"

I don't think Anthony ever lied in the past, and he doesn't really brag, so I guess his stories might have some *credibility.*

"Good buddies should give you a heads up which girls are doing it, except for maybe a real girlfriend. That's what truly good friends do!"

If nothing else, it would be nice to know which girls are doing it and how I can get them to do it with me.

14

Chapter Three

In contrast to Marc's experiences, Rhonda had benefitted from actual educational materials and long, detailed discussions and debates about sex and puberty with Gwen and a few other girlfriends during countless sleepovers over the years. When Rhonda was twelve, for example, her mom had given her a thirty-page booklet, *On Becoming a Woman*, which covered puberty, anatomical and hormonal changes, and the developmental basics of sex, birth control, and reproduction pretty well. Rhonda and Gwen voraciously devoured the booklet together and discussed all the very intriguing topics at great length, wondering when and how they would experience everything the book told them about.

They did the same thing when Gwen's mom gave her a similar book to read a few months later—Puberty: What Every Young Lady Needs to Know. They hungrily consumed it, page-by-page, point-by-point, soaking it in much more enthusiastically than any of their schoolwork.

However, although the booklets mentioned birth control, they certainly didn't describe how to actually use the different forms. They also didn't cover sexual diseases much, only briefly mentioning the well-known maladies of the time, such as syphilis and gonorrhea. Generally, the booklets' primary message about both birth control and sexual diseases was "be careful."

Chapter Four

"I don't find any of the boys in our ninth grade class to be especially cute, Gwen, and prefer guys who are a little older."

One Thursday morning in the crowded hall while changing classes, as Rhonda was talking with Gwen at her locker and both were discretely scanning the hall for cute guys, Marc appeared out of nowhere, like a dream.

All at once her general visual 'guy radar' antennae started to buzz, stopped, focused, and came to rest on Marc. Joking and laughing with a couple of his baseball buddies, twenty feet across the bustling and noisy hall, he became an irresistible draw.

In four months Marc would turn seventeen. He was known to most students to be a pretty good student and athlete, a guy who played second base on the junior varsity baseball team, and one who had started lifting weights. A few girls also knew him as smart, funny at times, a good kisser, and one of the more popular guys at school for all of those reasons.

When she first saw him, Rhonda knew none of this, of course—only that he was very cute, with a great smile and laugh, and fabulous dimples.

She was smitten. "Who *is* the incredibly cute guy in the green shirt?" she asked in a low voice, turning away from him so

Marc couldn't see the huge smile on her face and guess he was the focus of their conversation.

"Him?" Gwen asked tentatively. "Do you mean…like… the guy in the dark-green shirt?"

Getting Rhonda's quick nod, Gwen whispered into her best friend's ear, "I think his name is Marc, and like…I heard he's on the JV baseball team."

"He's *so* cute!" her horny neighbor murmured, excitement in her voice, looking quickly over her shoulder again at him and back to Gwen before he noticed.

Unable to stop smiling, Rhonda whispered it into Gwen's ear so nobody would hear, and Marc wouldn't know she was interested in him, yet. "Do you think he has…like… a girlfriend?"

"I don't know, but I think his sister, Jeannie, is …like…in our math class. I bet she'd know."

Upon hearing *that* very exciting news Rhonda decided right then to definitely make Marc's sister her friend as a means to learn everything possible to know about him. *The possibility Jeannie might introduce me to her brother is hugely exciting!*

Naturally positioning herself in the hall so she could look over Rhonda's shoulder in order to report on Marc's activities, or lack of activity, no matter where he moved, Gwen would appear to be conversing with her girlfriend.

"Is he looking this way?" Rhonda whispered excitedly.

Hoping he had noticed her, was glancing or smiling at her, or was even looking in her direction, Rhonda was mildly disappointed when it didn't happen.

Conceding Marc was cute, Gwen also concluded his tall, thin, blond buddy was just as cute. *I'm not going to compete with Rhonda for any guy because: A) I don't think I will win; B)*

I don't want any hard feelings between us; and C) there are plenty of cute guys to admire and fantasize about.

Over the next three weeks, Jeannie was surprised at all the questions Rhonda asked about her brother. She could see Rhonda had a crush on Marc and agreed to tell her most of the pertinent details about him *if* Rhonda would get an equal amount of surreptitious information about his taller, blond friend, Robby. Jeannie liked tall guys and in the last couple months had started noticing her brother's buddy with a romantic interest.

In junior and senior high, there was always a continuous flow of secret information about relationships and who liked who, so it was nothing out of the ordinary for the girls to pass information back and forth about the guys.

High school guys passed similar information back and forth about the girls, but most of it pertained to their past sexual history, current state of physical development, and present and future sexual potentials.

Knowing how gossip could easily get around, Gwen asked Rhonda, "Aren't you worried about...like... Jeannie telling Marc you're interested in him?"

"No, because if she does, I'll just tell Robby she likes him, and like...her secret would be out, too."

Two days later, Rhonda reported to Jeannie a cluster of pertinent information about Robby she learned from one of the girls on the JV cheerleading team: "He has only dated one girl once in the past. The rest of it—like, he's a pretty good athlete and student, usually gets...like... good grades, and eventually wants to become...like... a successful architect like his dad—you probably already know since he's been your brother's best friend since third grade. And, I'm sure you've noticed, like...he has *big hands*."

Big hands and big feet were supposed to be good indicators of a guy's cock-size, the girls had heard.

18

In response, Jeannie thanked Rhonda for her information and reported Marc had dated one girl casually, taking her twice to the movies, but currently didn't have a steady girlfriend; played second base on the baseball team; lifted weights; and was rumored to have probably made out with at least a couple girls.

Jeannie concluded her report with: "Marc's pretty smart and like...gets pretty good grades most of the time, mostly B's, wants to go to college, hopes for like...a baseball scholarship, and eventually has his mind set to be a professional baseball player."

Of course, being his sister, Marc's physical attributes were lost on Jeannie, but those details were all very obvious, and incredibly attractive, to Rhonda.

Collecting all the information she could gather without him knowing, it took Rhonda three more weeks to work up her courage to say hello to Marc in the hall while she was with Jeannie, Gwen, and some girlfriends they both knew, but he smiled briefly at her, in passing, which she found to be absolutely thrilling!

He smiled at me! Does that mean he noticed me? Maybe I have a chance with him!

When Rhonda and Gwen were alone later that day, Rhonda said, "I think he actually, like... noticed me. Do you think I should try to meet him somehow? Let's, like... come up with a plan!"

On Wednesday, when Jeannie casually mentioned she had overheard Marc talking to his buddies about going to the theater Saturday afternoon, a palpable shock went right through Rhonda, and she couldn't wait to tell Gwen the intriguing news. That night, the girls strategized, did some conversational role playing, and talked for hours about Saturday. Finally, the plan was set.

Chapter Five

Rhonda, Gwen, and Alice bumped into Marc and Robby in the lobby of the Essex Theater the next Saturday afternoon, hoping they made it look like it was completely by chance. The Essex Theater was a favorite destination for local teens. The high school guys called it the S-E-X Theater, of course.

Vaguely remembering Rhonda from the brief encounter in the hall with his sister, now Marc found himself glad to see her and zeroed in on her cute little figure and nice boobs right away. *She's a little young, but has a pretty nice body already—and more importantly, seems to be readily available.*

The "accidental" meeting at the theater snack bar led to a lot of giggling and nervous laughter on Rhonda's part as she was nervous about making a good impression. The group chatted about school, the athletic teams, favorite bands and music, the upcoming dance, some of the teachers, and a couple of the goofy kids, basically whatever Rhonda could think of from the mental list she'd prepared and rehearsed several times with Gwen.

Rhonda struggled to maintain eye contact with Marc without staring deep into his beautiful blue eyes and an uncontrollable ear-to-ear grin appearing.

I can't stop smiling! Damn! Stop!! Now!...it's no use...sigh...

Looking down at the floor and shifting from one foot to the other, she waited until her thoughts calmed and some semblance of control returned. *My stomach is doing flip-flops. Stop it!...Please!...*

Realizing Rhonda was struggling Gwen filled in the conversational gaps for her as best she could until her buddy regained her composure. It was also tough for her to think straight, herself, because seeing Robby made Gwen anxious too.

I'm dying to make a good impression. I desperately want Marc to like me! Rhonda thought.

She needn't have worried, though. His physical attraction to her was immediately strong. Liking what he saw, Marc knew the animal magnetism was mutual.

Marc is even cuter up close than I imagined. I can hardly speak I'm so nervous...and excited!

Finding they liked some of the same music and bands, The Beatles and The Righteous Brothers, her two favorite groups, pleased Rhonda and showed common shared musical tastes.

We have things in common.

Most important, Marc smiled at her.

What a great smile, with beautiful, straight, white teeth. And I like when it's directed at me! He has the deepest blue smiling eyes! I just can't *stop myself from grinning. Ugh! Stop! Please!...*

After about ten minutes of nervous conversation, the cartoons were starting, so Gwen, according to plan, excused herself and returned to the front row to sit with her younger sister. *Rhonda and I have, of course, agreed that I will disappear to give her more of his undivided time and attention.*

The naturally redheaded, Irish, perfect-complexioned, freckled ballet dancer with great legs and an edible ass, hazel-eyed Gwen O'Rourke, would get all the juicy details later.

What Rhonda and Gwen didn't know was that Marc and Robby also had a plan. Their agreement was pretty similar to the girls', in that if one of them looked like they were going to hook up with a girl, the other would make himself scarce.

It was no coincidence when Robby quietly disappeared.

Returning to her seat with Alice, Gwen was almost as excited as Rhonda and found it hard to concentrate on the screen, just thinking about what her girlfriend and Marc *might* be doing.

Noticing Gwen's excitement, Alice asked, "What are you all excited about? The movie hasn't even started yet. It's only the cartoons."

Alice is not quite fourteen and not old enough to share big-girl secrets yet. "Well, I like cartoons too, and this is supposed to be an excellent movie!"

Back in the lobby the conversation was awkward and halting.

"Well…um….I have never…I mean…I don't really know…" Rhonda's voice nervously stammered then trailed off to nothing. Trying again, "Where do…uh…like…you usually… sit, Marc?

My voice refuses to speak like I want! Crap! "Where…um…is the best… place…to…like…see…?"

Her hesitant and uncomfortable assertion she didn't know the best place to sit because it was her first visit was…simply ridiculous. Rhonda had been there dozens of times. But she had

22

been younger, and her agendas then were much different, a fact Marc didn't have to know anyway.

"Well…um…Rhonda…er…"

There's only her and I left, now…so…I can see she's struggling to talk…too…so…maybe it means she's as nervous as I am.

Taking a calculated risk, Marc smiled, and invited her to sit with him, far away from the guy he came with, in the darkest part of the theater, on the left side. It was the section of the theater commonly known as The Playground, the make-out area.

"My buddy, Robby, likes to sit in the…uh… front row but … like…its too close for me 'cause you have to look almost straight up the entire movie. Sure…um… uh…you can see clearly, but my neck gets stiff after a while. I …like…uh…know a better place."

"You know…a better place than…the front row, Marc?"

"Yeah. About fifteen rows back on the left side…um… its pitch black, which helps you see the picture better, and…er…you don't get a stiff neck! That's where I like to sit. Want to…like… try it out with me? You'll see…"

"Well…I guess so…if you say it's like…better…Marc…"

Great! She's agreeable! A possible make-out girl!

It *was* the darkest area. Pitch black. That much was true.

Marc and Robby had come to the movie in search of girls, and now this potential make-out girl had found *him*, without any effort on his part. They'd visited this movie theater two other times with his baseball buddies in the past month without any success even meeting, let alone making out with, girls.

The guys suspected but didn't know for sure the girls came there hunting for guys, too, although it *could have been* just a lucky, chance encounter. The girls got the benefit of the doubt.

Robby realized too late he had missed the opportunity to take Gwen to The Playground, too. The possibility didn't dawn on him until after the movie. Happy for Marc, though, he hoped to get the whole scoop later, if anything exciting happened with Rhonda.

Secretly hoping Robby would also ask her to sit with him too, Gwen was so nervous and excited already about Rhonda's hookup there was a little relief, and perhaps a little disappointment, when Robby didn't ask her. *Maybe it'll happen next time, **if** there is a next time.*

The Playground was always very dark because the high school guys made a point of frequently removing or breaking the aisle lights in that left-hand section. On weekends, in fact, there were usually *no* functioning left-aisle lights.

Knowing the area and its reputation from the other older girls at school, she was very much hoping Marc would invite her there. *I really don't need convincing, either, because it has been my plan all along. I just don't want to appear too eager.*

He wasn't inviting her there for the picture quality, she knew. *Marc wants to make out with me and even the* thought *of it is making my heart pound, my hands sweaty, and I can barely breathe!*

"It's dark, so be careful. Come this way with me, Rhonda."

Taking Rhonda's hand, Marc led her thru the pitch-black darkness down the aisle to a seat fifteen rows towards the screen and ten seats in from the aisle.

Immediately Rhonda knew she liked him holding her hand, for starters, even though her hands were a little sweaty from all the nervous excitement.

This is the first time I've ever held hands with a boy I like! It's so romantic!

Marc's hands were sweaty, too, but he kept wiping them quickly on his pants when they got too wet, hoping she wouldn't notice. *I like holding her soft, warm hands. Wonder if she will mind me putting my arm around her shoulders? That'll be my first move, a trial run to see how she reacts.*

It took both of them a minute to let their eyes adjust to the darkness, but once Rhonda could see, she delightedly discovered Marc's arm already around the back of her seat, slowly sliding down to her shoulders. Her heart rate wildly shot up. *Oh my God! It's happening! Marc has his arm around me, and he's running his fingers lightly thru my hair! It feels great to have him touch me like that!*

Marc thought it was pretty great, too. *Putting my arm around Rhonda feels good, like I am protecting her to some extent, even though there's no apparent danger present at the time, except for maybe me and my incredible urges!*

Noticing the faint scent of his aftershave, she smiled, even though it would quickly become apparent his cheeks were pretty smooth and probably didn't really need shaving much at all at sixteen-and-a-half years old.

So far, it's all happening as I hoped it would, Marc realized. Turning to her he whispered with a smile, "Your hair smells great, Rhonda. It feels *so* soft!"

Jeez, there is his nice, big, beautiful smile again! Responding with a weak smile of her own.

Marc was happy to see that she liked his compliment. *And I'm not giving her a line—her soft hair really does smell clean, fresh, and flowery!*

Rhonda's curiosities about guys, what they felt like, smelled like, and how they tasted, were running wild. *I've discussed a million details about guys for hours on sleepovers with Gwen, but now I actually can find out for real! And it isn't just any spin-the-bottle guy; it's unbelievably adorable **Marc**!*

Still somewhat nervous, he could tell she liked him by her nervous laughter, shy but constant smile, and constant inability to look him in the eye for more than a second without smiling. *I can't believe how I lucked out. This girl is cute, has a nice figure, and is apparently willing to let me touch her, which makes her perfect for me because those are the only three things I really require in a girl.*

His curiosity about girls equaled her questions about guys: what they smelled like, felt like, and how they tasted.

So far so good, he thought.

Pretending to watch the movie, Rhonda found it hard to concentrate with Marc's hands in her hair. Her excitement growing, she became impatient waiting for whatever was going to happen next, glancing nervously in his direction a couple times, and then quickly back toward the screen.

Is he going to kiss me, or not? Please! Kiss me! I'm dying!

Going for broke, Marc turned her head toward him and leaned over to kiss her mouth. *She's letting me kiss her! How cool!* Her soft, warm mouth offered no resistance, but her lips were closed and temporarily resisted his tongue pushing into her mouth.

I want to give her some tongue, but if she really resists, I'll be almost as happy just to kiss her soft lips.

Fortunately the resistance was minimal.

On Marc's third attempt, Rhonda relented and let him push his tongue in a little, then all the way. *She tastes like cherries—soft, warm, willing, juicy, cherries. My tongue is in her mouth! Oh man, I can feel her tongue playing with mine! We are French kissing!*

Rhonda was ecstatic to finally be French kissing a boy. It was kind of like practicing with Gwen but somehow more exciting. Her heart started pounding; her senses reeling. *He actually wants to kiss me!* Feared she might faint as his mouth and tongue pressed hers, touching her lips, tasting her, Rhonda began to feel weak, wet, and wonderful at the same time, without any desire to resist him, even if the longing was there, which it wasn't.

Impossibly cute and kisses great, too! God yes! YES!

Chapter Six

Marc is the fourth guy I have ever kissed, and the first I really like and plan to spend much time alone with, making out.

Kissing in general was enjoyable, Rhonda had already found. In addition to her initial exploratory sessions with Gwen, she had some kissing experience with boys, too. While playing spin-the-bottle a party last year, she had kissed three boys, but those kisses only lasted a minute or so and were the luck-of-the-bottle draw, not really with boys she especially liked. *This time is different. This is Marc, my first real potential beau.*

Continuing to kiss, Rhonda thought about how much she liked the feel of his tongue inside her mouth. *It's the first time I have been entered by a guy in any way, and it feels nice, even kind of natural.* A warm, pleasurable, possibly sexual flush spread all over her body while they were kissing, which scared her a little. *I wonder if it's possible to feel too good.* Several more minutes of passionate French kissing, holding their breath for long intervals, left them both panting and out of breath.

How are you supposed to breathe while kissing, through your nose? Whew! She's panting, too. Good! It's not just me!

Rhonda needed a break to gather her senses about her before she simply threw herself down flat in the theater chair and asked him to screw right there. *Granted, it's a lovely and lustfully*

28

romantic thought, and certainly in my future sexual plans, but not on a first date! I don't want Marc to think I'm a slut!

Rhonda found out the other girls had been right: *Marc really is a great kisser! He makes it feel so good, and seems to like it as much as I do!* She liked not only feeling his lips on hers, but also being able to feel the hardening muscles of his arms around her and of his chest against her breasts.

I'm really tickled the making out is going so well, with no noses bumped into, or other embarrassing incidents. The warm willing softness of her lips and the soft warmth of her body against mine feel great. Both have a lot of future potential.

Marc liked the way her body felt against his, too, and he was glad nothing embarrassing or awkward had happened yet, like bumping noses or gnashing teeth. *She seems willing enough, and has a lot of so-far unrealized potential, so I plan to gradually test her limits, to see what she will allow.*

After gathering her senses, taking several deep breaths, and regaining some sense of control for a few minutes, while making awkward superficial conversation about the movie they were missing, Rhonda felt Marc turn her head toward him, and once again locked his lips to hers. All at once, those warm and willing, tingling sensations deep inside returned and grew, as her initial resolve to set some physical and sexual boundaries wilted away.

"Let me…get this…out…of...the…"

Pulling the armrest between the seats up and out of the way, Marc turned his whole upper body to face her. Rhonda shifted to face him too, and they were in a wonderful, sexually charged embrace with no barrier between them before she knew it.

Pulling her to his chest in a big hug, Marc could feel her breasts and body against him. Warm and electrifying feelings travelled in both directions. Receiving no protest, he kissed her

29

again, hands cupping her face gently, and then dropped his right hand slowly lower from her jaw down her neck to her waiting breast, giving her plenty of time to stop him if she wanted.

I don't want to stop him because it feels fantastic. Oh my God! He wants to touch me! Marc thinks I'm attractive, maybe even sexy! The warm feelings from kissing him were now beginning to get warmer, more and more tingly, and juicier, as they drifted downward. *Even the **idea** of Marc touching my breast is almost as exciting as the actual touch.*

Almost.

When Marc actually copped a feel of her almost fully developed boobs thru her blouse and her bra, making out suddenly became considerably more exciting. *At least he's just touching me through my blouse and bra. In fact, I'm glad I'm wearing a bra—it gives me another line of defense against my own raging desires! If he starts to go under my blouse and unhook my bra, do I want him to stop? Should I cross that line and let him do that?*

After making out for a while, Rhonda knew she liked it and liked him. Wanting to please him and herself at the same time, a definite conflict was created regarding what to do next.

I also don't want him to think I am a total tramp by screwing him the first time we meet! Besides, she didn't have a rubber, didn't know if Marc owned one, and had no desire for that question to surface. *There is no way I want him to suspect I am even thinking about rubbers the first time we're together!*

From Marc's perspective, things were going very well, indeed. *Rhonda is even more willing than I'd hoped, and she didn't even try to stop me when I felt her boobs through her clothes. I just know things will be even better if I can get her blouse unbuttoned.* What he would do then wasn't clear, but Marc knew he wanted to slide his hand inside her bra, a first for him. *First base! Yes-s! I wonder if her tips are stiff, like my dick is now.*

Even through her blouse and bra he could already enjoy the soft, warm sponginess of her breast. *Wonder if she'll let me get to first base? Just like on the ball field, you gotta get to first base to even have any chance of scoring. And then you have to touch all the bases to score!*

Bras were a mystery to him, but one he fully intended to solve. *They're an obstacle to be overcome, somehow, and removed or bypassed on the way to even better things.*

When Marc tried to unbutton her blouse, Rhonda put her hand on his to stop him. *I'm almost positive it would feel too good,* she told herself. Not wanting to discourage him *too* much, she distracted him in a last ditch effort by giving the intriguing bulge in his pants a nice, firm squeeze, causing him to groan deeply.

Hooray! This is my first actual, 100%, without-a-doubt hard-on! I did it! The pleasure in having created his hard-on, her first she knew of for sure, as a potentially sexual female, sexual partner, lover, possible future girlfriend, and eventual mate, was immense!

Hearing Marc's groan, Rhonda knew he liked where her hand was, gripping him, but she was a little disappointed for herself as it had distracted him from groping her breasts.

Moving his hand on top of hers, in his lap, Marc gave her firm grip on him a friendly squeeze. *Feeling her boobs through her clothes is great, but I like her hand on my cock even more.* When Rhonda didn't pull her hand away, he whispered, "Take it out," but her hands were trembling and she didn't respond, although her hand did not quit gripping him, either.

Uh oh, I've fantasized about unzipping a guy's pants, but I've never done it before. I'm sure it'll take two hands to get the zipper down. It didn't really matter, though, because her sweaty, trembling hands were too unsteady to unzip him in the dark, anyway.

Beyond the problem of getting Marc's pants unzipped, Rhonda thought about what she had heard about a guy's underwear. *I wonder if it really has an opening in the front for easy access. Can I find it in the dark if I feel around for it? I will be so embarrassed if I can't find it! I'm so nervous! My stomach is quivering inside, and my hands are shaking too much! Stop!*

Unable to control his rapid heart rate or nervousness, either, things were going even better than Marc had hoped, so the decision to act was quickly made.

Moving Rhonda's hand to the side, onto his leg, he held the top of his zipper with his right hand, and unzipped his fly with the left, pulling his erect cock thru the small hole in the front of his underwear for her to feel, just as she hoped.

Unspoken but welcome relief flooded both of them.

Seeing his member emerge rigid from his pants, Rhonda remained too nervous and unsure to act, so Marc returned her hand from his leg to where it was before, gently gripping his stiff dick.

Oh My God! His cock is freaking beautiful! I can't believe it!

Amazed and surprised how hard and stiff it became in her grasp, she marveled how smooth it was at the same time, overall, with the tip being the softest part. *What a wondrous thing! It's responding to my touch and even pointing toward me in a nice, friendly, sexy way. My first official, freakin beautiful warm smooth hard-on is in my hand!*

32

Squeezing it gently a couple times, Rhonda elicited another groan from Marc, but wasn't really sure what to do next. *Okay, I've heard most guys like their cocks rubbed up and down, gently but firmly, top to bottom, slow and fast... so here goes...*

Massaging it slowly up and down, Rhonda wasn't sure at first if she was doing it right or not, but assumed something must be going okay as long as he was continuing to groan and stay hard.

I'm pleasing and pleasuring Marc! I am doing it! Yes-s!

Closing his eyes Marc enjoyed her hand massage for a full three minutes before taking the next step.

This is fucking great! Are all girls' hands this soft?

"Give it a kiss..." he whispered hoarsely, and hopefully.

This hand massage is great, but her lips on it would be even better . . . !

There were no bad choices. It was a win-win situation.

Rhonda liked kissing Marc and was pretty sure she would like kissing his cock, too. Wanting badly to kiss, feel, and smell it, she also feared, however, he might want her to suck it, too. *Only slutty and easy girls suck it on the first date! That is* not *the first impression I want to make!*

She was actually looking forward to sucking it with great anticipation and excitement, however, because it would be the first time a cock entered any part of her body, and the very thought, alone, was thrilling! Oral sex would be the next exciting step, another milestone in her sexual awakening.

If his cock is in my mouth, it's pretty safe—I can't get pregnant from that.

The sexual education class in eighth grade had taught her about how birth control and a little about sexually transmitted diseases, so Rhonda knew to look for sores or any funny smells from a guy's dick as potential signs of a problem, making him a male to be avoided.

Not seeing or feeling any sores on Marc's cock or detecting any odd smells, after giving it a few quick, light kisses and licks up and down, top to bottom, bottom to top, she returned to her manual full-length frequent firm soft and sensual stroking.

God yes, does this feel fucking great! She's like warm silk.

Eyes closed, his breathing fast and deep, Marc was groaning frequently as Rhonda smoothly massaged him up and down, slow and fast, gently and firmly.

Her eyes were wide open, however. *I don't want to miss anything about the entire experience with him, especially his squirt! I **hope** he squirts! It will be my **first** cum shot!*

Wanting to satisfy Marc but had no idea how long it would take to do it, Rhonda continued her warm, manual massage, switching hands when one got tired, interspersing passionate kisses and light, long licks along the shaft, top to bottom, bottom to top.

His cock seems to be about five or six inches long, which I guess is about average, from what I've heard from my girlfriends. Of course, I don't really care how long it is—it's the first stiff cock I've ever held in my hands, it's mine for now, and it's simply beautiful!

From time to time Rhonda tried various grips on him to see which ones worked best, light, firm, and medium-firm hand pressures along with fast, slow, and medium-paced rhythms. *Most of those combinations seem to please him. I'll try different stroking techniques, caresses, licks, and kisses so I can tell which ones please him most. Kisses and licks give my hands a rest, too.*

Immersing herself in the long-awaited learning process, Rhonda eagerly yet quietly asked, "Does that feel good, Marc?" …groan…"What about *this*?...louder and deeper responses…!"

I'm probably looking forward to his orgasm just as much as he is! My hands are getting tired, though, and if he doesn't ejaculate soon I'll be forced to suck it, which she was looking forward to trying, but at a later time as a very special treat for both of them. *Sucking it will be my last resort if the hand job isn't successful. I'm going to* **love** *sucking his cock—I just know it!*

Male orgasms were something Rhonda had heard about and assumed his would be similar to her own, with pleasures building one on top of another until relief and release could no longer be resisted and a tsunami of rhythmic contractions would wash over her, causing her to groan loudly and stiffening her entire body for several seconds, or more, after which she would gradually relax, sated for the time being.

Masturbating since age twelve on an almost daily basis, Rhonda found she was multi-orgasmic, meaning she could achieve orgasm several times, one after the other, when the mood was right and there was proper physical and mental stimulation. Posters of her favorite teen idols or rockers, an active imagination, dim lighting, and romantic ballads on the radio or the record player helped fuel her fantasies, lighting the fire of her passions.

Soapy orgasms in the shower are great, too, but twice I almost fainted from the intensity, so those in my bed late at night suit me better, before dropping off into a fully relaxed and incredibly satisfying sleep.

Surprising as it was, Rhonda discovered almost half of her girlfriends were not multi-orgasmic, and some of them did not even admit to getting themselves off every day. *Those girls are really missing out on opportunities to enjoy an ability given to them by their Creator to experience all the incredibly pleasurable sensations possible. I'll definitely **not** make that mistake!* She assured herself.

She and her girlfriends were pretty sure very few, if any, guys were multi-orgasmic, but Rhonda imagined male orgasms would be as satisfying as her own. *My orgasms are very wet, warm, and oh-so satisfying but did not really erupt like I imagine, anticipate, and hope Marc's will soon be.*

Just thinking about or saying the words *e-jac-u-la-tion* and *or-gasm* were arousing to Rhonda. And when those words were applied to Marc, specifically, the current object of her teenage desires, her excitement increased exponentially.

My heart is pounding so hard I can barely think! I want him to ejaculate bad! I hope I'm doing this right. If this first cum shot goes well I hope it will be the first of many in the future for us!

She was not the only one eagerly anticipating his climax.

Christ, does this feel good! Rhonda's doing pretty well, so far. Her hands feel good, and they are hitting some real good spots. She hasn't quite got the rhythm just how I like it yet, but it still feels so great overall I can't stop groaning! Hell yeah! Jack me off! Take it all Rhonda! Milk me dry! Oh Yeah! It's all yours!

Of course, he also was aware, like most guys, any hand job was a good hand job, in the beginning, just like any feel of a female breast was a good feel, no matter what size her breast was. *It's all good. I wonder if she's enjoying giving me a hand job as much as I'm enjoying receiving it. This is my first time a girl's given me a hand job, after giving myself dozens in the past. I didn't realize her hands would feel so soft and warm! Are all girls this soft? Is she this soft all over?*

After almost five minutes of incredibly exciting manual massage, Marc gave a low and strong growl, his whole body tensed, and a strong squirt of thick, white semen erupted six inches straight up into the air, falling on Rhonda's hand and his pants, splattering seminal fluid all over the place.

Groan! God yes! I can't take any more pleasure! She has done me in! It feels SO goood!

Yes! YES! YES!!! Rhonda exclaimed silently, in her mind. *I did it! We did it! Marc has shot his wad!*

Perpetrating this eruptive miracle, Rhonda was initially amazed, proud, and very pleased, her first magnificent and oh-so-pleasing ejaculation. *I'm probably just as thrilled as Marc!*

Her elation, pride, and amazement in herself and her accomplishment unfortunately caused her to stop massaging him after the first squirt, thinking she and he were done, which meant Marc had to draw out the last couple squirts himself, manually.

Oh no! I'm making a real mess! But she stopped! I'll have to finish this rush myself! Why did she stop before I finished?

One shot was exciting to both of them, two shots would be twice as good, and three shots would finish the magic trifecta!

Honestly not knowing how many squirts to expect... *Two? Three? More?...* It turned out that three was the magic number and what she was hoping for. *The more the better! I want it all!*

Her pride in satisfying him turned to slight disappointment when she realized he wasn't finished, and watched Marc coax the last two remaining shots with his own hand.

Deciding then and there, Rhonda vowed in the future to continue her manual massage until he stopped squirting, with a minimum of three spurts. *Marc has more than one gift for me. I want and will take all he has.*

She was learning fast.

A *little* disappointed Rhonda didn't finish him off like he wanted, Marc wasn't about to complain. *One free orgasmic shot is way better than none, but maybe I can teach her another time—if there is another time—that at least three great spasms is the norm, the ultimate goal, for me anyway. In any case, at this point I'm very pleasantly drained and exhausted, so I can't really complain.*

Glancing around, once he let it fly, the first thing Rhonda did after he let it go was to scan the theater to determine if anyone had heard Marc's strong orgasmic groan and growl, but there were no apparent sounds or sights in the darkness moving their way, so she relaxed some.

Whew! So far, so good. Damn, that was freakin' great!

If someone *had* come to check out the situation, it would have been impossible to hide what had been going on. The ejaculate had flown everywhere. It smelled and felt like nothing she had ever experienced before. *Its so sticky, slick, and well...*masculine *is the only way to describe it.*

The strong smell was undeniable, and Rhonda liked it, but it also would have been painfully obvious to anybody else, especially any adult, who investigated.

I definitely don't like being in this exposed and vulnerable, position. Sex and orgasms are private happenings, to be shared only with special people, like Marc, and are nobody else's business.

Rhonda also knew her parents would be really upset if they found out what she had been doing in the theater.

Still, she viewed the gooey stuff all over her hands to be a beautiful mess—*my first experience with semen, the amazing substance that can one day, when I am ready, make me pregnant, and a mother with a family of my own. One day I will combine his gift with mine, making us both parents.*

Although feeling very good about herself and Marc as a possible new couple. Rhonda knew in the back of her mind there were also possible emotional disappointments to be considered once you crossed the line into more adult romantic relationships, but she quickly chose to damper those for now and focus on the positive, exhilarating, and incredibly satisfying sexual aspects, instead.

This new experience for Rhonda was both exciting and scary at the same time.

Exciting, because I'm entering a different type of relationship than ever before, with a guy—emotionally and physically. Scary, because I know with sexual activity also is the very real possibility of pregnancy and sexual diseases. Since pregnancy is certainly not in my immediate plans while frequent sex and lovemaking are, obvious precautions will have to be taken.

Marc felt about the same way and had some of the same concerns as Rhonda, but as a guy he didn't view the pregnancy issue quite the same way. *I want to be very sexual with Rhonda, but don't want to have to deal with any pregnancy or sexually transmitted disease worries, either. I definitely need a rubber, or preferably, a bunch of them!*

Focused mainly on the pleasurable sexual aspects of life, Marc was fascinated with the process of exploring and enjoying females, and learning more about them, although he was not averse in any way to them exploring him if they wanted, too.

Two-way exploration, pleasure, and mutual, simultaneous satisfaction were the ideal goals.

Is Rhonda mad because I made a mess all over the place? Marc wondered. *She doesn't appear very upset, though.* For a few moments, he was a little concerned, like her, somebody might come over to investigate, expose, and embarrass the hell out of both of them, but his worry soon subsided.

Taking a deep breath, he allowed himself to surrender to the relaxing satisfaction flooding thru his veins.

I'm also somewhat concerned about having my limp, messy cock out in public, but I'm too drained to do anything about it. Marc had never thought that far ahead to plan how the clean-up consequences should be handled in a situation like this. His hormonal interests and mental processes basically stopped at the end of his dick.

Chapter Seven

Putting all other reverie aside, her practical side returned and Rhonda wondered what she should do now. *Marc has dropped off to sleep with a mess in his lap and all over my hands. Who cleans up?*

First, however, Rhonda *knew* she had to taste the sticky stuff to satisfy her own curiosity. So, after tentatively giving her fingers a quick lick, she was pleasantly surprised to find the taste was slightly salty and kind of milky, but not as yucky as she had heard. *It's slippery, smooth, and slick to my tongue, but doesn't taste horrible, like some other girls have told me.*

An older, more experienced girl once remarked to Gwen, who passed it on to Rhonda, the theory that semen was the glue which kept couples together. She liked the thought, whether the girl had been kidding or not, and was determined to find out if it was true. *If it is true, I plan to make Marc and his cum my friend.*

The fact this fluid had been inside him only seconds ago and was now hers for the taking, as a gift she could safely take inside herself, overrode all of her other concerns and reservations. *Taking it in my mouth is a way to accept his semen inside me without having to worry about getting pregnant,* she figured, *even though I know there is always a miniscule possibility of getting an STD like herpes or gonorrhea orally.*

So Rhonda began lingually cleaning him and herself, hiding the evidence of their intimate moment together. *It'll eliminate the possibility of being discovered, and will be* our *secret. A very important and magical part of Marc will now be inside of me.*

Licking and sucking the semen off her hand and fingers, Rhonda gently took his now limp, and somewhat safe, cock in her mouth to suck it clean. *Even a flaccid, slippery, spent dick in my mouth is very exciting! It's the first time I have ever experienced a cock inside me in any way!*

And the now-shriveled cock belonged to Marc, which made it even more fabulous to her. Finishing the job Rhonda next wiped his pants with a six-inch-square, white, silk handkerchief she had brought in her purse, specifically for this possible occasion. Once he was clean she put the cloth very carefully back in her purse. *It'll serve later as evidence when I relay all the juicy details to Gwen.*

Although Rhonda conceded some girls might be turned off by the idea, she knew her best girlfriend pretty well, and was very sure Gwen would be excited, curious, and thrilled, as the hanky full of Marc would provide both of them with an electrifying first experience- first smell and taste of a guy's semen, the sharing of which Rhonda knew would be almost as thrilling as when it was collected earlier.

Gwen will freakin love it! I just know it! I will also be bragging a little bit! ...I know...I know...!

It was a luscious secret to keep, but they might tell a select girlfriend, too, and then Rhonda would be in a very special, and growing, secret category of girls—a Girl Who Has Actually Had Sex, in Some Form, Successfully.

42

Chapter Eight

Although Marc was not fully asleep, he had exhaustedly sunken into his seat and was not moving at all, except to utter the occasional moan or sigh.

The only thing he knew at the moment was the feeling of being pleasantly drained, and weak. *Wow! Rhonda has drained me dry, without me doing much of anything. What a great start! Wonder if she'll do it every day? Twice a day? Three times? Whenever I want?* That *would be freakin' fabulous!*

And then the experience unexpectedly got even better.

Now she is licking me clean and swallowing it! She swallows—I don't believe it! And it feels so good. Rhonda is doing it exactly how I hoped she would. If I could summon some energy, even a few molecules, I would thank her. This is unbelievable!

The hand job was great, but messy, so in the future Marc decided he would try to convince Rhonda to jack him off into her mouth and swallow every time. *It'll be even cooler if Rhonda is willing to swallow it directly from my cock, without making a mess first!*

Marc knew he liked making out with Rhonda and wanted to do it every day, but would have to find a better place to do it—*I*

43

certainly can't afford to go to the movies all the time. The forest, which is close to both of our homes, might give us some privacy, and it's free.

It was March and spring was coming on, but it was still only in the high forties at night, so a blanket would probably be necessary in the forest, Marc figured.

Rhonda knew she liked Marc, liked being with him, laughing and talking with him, kissing and making out with him, jacking him off, and satisfying him, even though it did make a mess afterward. *I definitely want to be his steady sex partner and maybe even his girlfriend.*

There was no doubt in her mind she liked bringing Marc to climax. *It's a power I have never possessed before, even though I have fantasized about it many times. It's a sexual power. Now I know for sure I can do it successfully.* Her intrinsic female sexual power was very exciting in itself, but the fact she could use her blossoming sensuality specifically to please and satisfy *Marc* tripled the thrill!

Until now, the only real sexual power I've enjoyed is pleasuring myself, which is pretty satisfying, but there isn't any romance or relationship to it, except in my frequent fantasies.

She also appreciated her great relationship with Gwen, which was exciting and pleasurable in a different way, but Rhonda wanted a real romantic relationship with Marc.

Thinking of Marc brought her back to the present and how she had dealt with the messiness problem as a result of his orgasm. She decided then and there to make a quick and clean act of it in the future by swallowing the evidence as it made its appearance. *My pleasing and satisfying Marc pleases and satisfies me, too.*

Rhonda loved thinking Marc found her attractive, as well. She was pretty sure he'd liked making out with her so far—kissing her, playing with her breasts, ejaculating from her manual massage. As a result of all those positive developments, she began mentally planning what to do with him in future encounters.

If I allow Marc to cum in my mouth, there won't be any mess or any evidence of what we have been doing. I can't wait to feel his cock squirting his sexy semen into my mouth. I already love making him hard, hearing him moan, and knowing I'm pleasuring him. Once his cum is quickly swallowed and completely inside me, it'll be a very private, intimate, and special secret we'll share.

Some older girls in her school who had successfully given blowjobs had warned her about letting a guy cum into the back of her throat, which could make her choke and gag. *The solution to that problem is to deflect his sperm with the tip of my tongue on the tip of his cock.* Rhonda thought she could master the technique with some practice.

One day pretty soon, when the time is right, I will welcome a cock, hopefully Marc's, inside me in an even sexier way, but I'll make sure I'm on the Pill or otherwise protected, and/or he'll wear a rubber. Our joining will be the ultimate joy, to be as one with Marc, making love, but that's still a ways down the romantic and sexual road. I simply can't wait!

Rhonda's past questions about guys, cocks, kissing, romance, tastes, smells, breast feels, embraces, hard-ons, and semen were being answered. *The fact I like Marc and it seems to be mutual makes it even more special.*

After Marc recovered a bit, Rhonda leaned over and whispered in his ear, "I *really do* want to learn how to do it, Marc, so…whenever you want to shoot your load in the future, just let me know. I will make sure our evidence disappears right away, next time, into my stomach."

I'm excited to use the term "our" because it implies we are a couple. It's surprising to me how quickly I've developed a special affection for him.

Marc was very groggy but also very surprised and pleased to hear her fulfilling his unspoken wish, and managed to give her an affectionate glancing kiss on the forehead. *I can't believe my good luck, to find a girl who will swallow without even being asked. How cool! Life is good! I didn't even have to ask her!*

From Rhonda's perspective, she wanted to be special to him, to be his girlfriend, and was pretty sure no other girls had made him any similar offers. *I want everything he has to offer.*

Marc didn't even notice her use of "our". He didn't pick up on what it signified to Rhonda, especially in his drained state.

All he could think was, *Hey, I'm horny, and if she wants to make out, let me play with her boobs, and eventually swallow a load of my semen, for whatever reason, I'm certainly not going to argue with her.*

Somehow, it just felt like the right, safe, and natural thing for him, and her, to do. He was a little concerned maybe she was doing it just to please him, as a sexual favor for which he would later be obligated in some way. *Is a girl who swallows your cum necessarily your girlfriend? How many times does she swallow it before you have to declare her your girlfriend? Ten? Five? Twenty?*

It was all so cool. *Is it possible girls are as curious about guys as guys are curious about girls? I've no idea, but I hope so.*

Whatever her reasons were, Marc wasn't going to debate or argue with her. It was a normal turn of events. *There's just something exciting and satisfying about having my cock, and*

46

cum, safely inside her, without having to worry about her getting pregnant. Seems like a safe, satisfying, sexual experience to me. What a great start!

Of the three girls Marc had made out with in the past, Rhonda was the best kisser and had the nicest boobs. He was also glad she smelled so nice and had such soft lips and hands.

Hearing her say she will swallow the evidence in the future is VERY *cool, too, because most girls I've heard of don't like tasting or swallowing it at all, and some just flat out refuse. Now I don't have to ask her to swallow, or argue, or try to persuade her, because she already volunteered. How cool is that? I sometimes masturbate three or four times a day. Shooting my load in Rhonda's soft, warm, sexy mouth three or four times a day will be* way *cooler! One of my biggest and best fantasies is coming to be!*

Marc could kind of understand why some girls didn't want to perform oral sex. *I don't think I'd be too keen on getting a mouthful of semen, either. I know how messy it is when I jack off, but also know how much personal pleasure and satisfaction I get from it.* Now, since Rhonda seemed to like bringing him to orgasm, too, it would be even better to share it. Things were progressing nicely.

Me, my cock, and my cum are a package deal. Any girl who doesn't like my cock or cum doesn't really like me because it is a very important part of me, and brings me great pleasure and satisfaction! Rhonda seems to like all of me!

None of the other prior girls had ever given him a hand job, so Marc definitely liked Rhonda best because she did, was available, and willing. *She doesn't even seem to care about the mess. Hell, she even finished wiping it up with her own handkerchief!*

Now that he'd gotten a feel of Rhonda's breasts, Marc was anxious to get an eventual taste of them. Pussy, of course, would be even more interesting, and exciting, from his perspective, because it was unknown, mysterious, and so potentially awesome and satisfying to explore, get into and fully enjoy. *I can't wait to enjoy touching her warm, yielding, mysterious feminine inner softness.*

This line of thought brought his mind right back to his baseball analogies. *Second and third base—yes! Second base is one step closer to scoring, and third base is even closer to home plate! Home plate, here I come, literally and figuratively!* He thought, smiling at his own witticism.

The horny, hormonal part of him wanted to satisfy his strong need for daily release by ejaculating in her somewhere, anywhere! *Until I can hit a home run, her soft warm sexy mouth will be an excellent alternative option!*

Additionally, they could hide any future sexual activities from their parents more easily that way. *Once she swallows it, the evidence is safely gone, never to return. Rhonda will know it and I will know it. That's enough for now, although I'll probably tell at least one of my buddies about this!! I can't believe my good luck!*

He also liked the fact Rhonda let him know she planned to have some form of sex with him in the future. She suggested making plans Monday, at school, but Marc didn't want to miss a day without getting his rocks off, so he suggested a call tomorrow, Sunday, to set up another meeting, maybe in the forest. *I need daily relief!*

Rhonda excitedly agreed. *Marc is missing me already!*

Chapter Nine

When Rhonda returned to Gwen and Alice in the front-row theater seats that Saturday afternoon, her BFF was anxiously awaiting her return to, first, make sure she was okay and, second, to get her to share each and every detail of everything that had happened with Marc.

Rhonda also wanted to share each minute detail with Gwen because it had been *so* exciting, thrilling, fun, epic, awesome, exhilarating…she'd need a whole thesaurus full of words to describe it. *Basically, it's the best day of my life! Without a doubt!*

Over the years Gwen was generally thrilled and excited to be sharing Rhonda's social and sexual escapades vicariously, although there may have been a hint of jealousy and envy flashing across her face, at times, it usually quickly disappeared.

Chapter Ten

This was all so cool Marc was just bursting to tell someone. *Man, it's like a wet dream is coming true!* Marc's buddy Robby, an outfielder on the baseball team, was the logical choice. They had grown up together and knew they could basically trust each other. Deciding to tell Robby later, after swearing him to silence, he was pretty sure his buddy wouldn't believe him. *I wouldn't blame him if he doesn't believe it, because it is pretty unbelievable, but I've got to tell somebody!*

After the movie, as Robby and Marc were riding their bikes home, they stopped at the baseball diamond and sat in the deserted bleacher seats to discuss the Essex afternoon.

"Okay, dude, out with it!" Robby demanded. "How was it? Did you score at all? First base? What? Or were you shutout?"

"Don't tell anybody, Robby… but it was absolutely fucking fabulous!"

"Does that mean you got to first base, or not?"

"Kinda…"

"Kinda? What the hell does 'kinda' mean? Either you did or you didn't! Which is it? Or are you gonna play it cutesy all day?"

Leaning closer, Marc spoke in a softer voice and lower volume. "She has really nice boobs. I didn't actually get to feel her boobs, but I did feel them thru her blouse!"

"Well, was it just a quick feel, and she stopped you, or not?"

"She didn't stop me at all! We were kissing and I felt her up! Rhonda is so soft and warm! I never realized how soft and warm girls are! Her lips, her boobs—everything!"

"Damn! I should have put a move on her girlfriend, Gwen, the redhead! Horny girls stick together."

"I'm hoping Rhonda is as horny as me! Man, it would be cool to get off every day with her. Getting another hand job, at least, will be the ticket!"

"*Another* hand job? What the fuck? You didn't tell me anything about any hand job! Spill the beans, you lucky shit!"

"Well, I was getting to that part...Rhonda wouldn't let me unbutton her shirt or put my hand inside, but didn't mind me squeezing her boobs thru her blouse. And then she didn't hesitate to grab my dick!

"She actually grabbed your dick? Are you just bullshitting me? Did she give you a hand job or not? A blowjob?"

"Hey, dude, I swear it all happened just like I'm telling you! I'm *not* lying!"

"Making out the first time you meet a broad is very possible, but feeling her up *and* getting a hand job is hard to believe, don't you think? You actually want me to *believe* that?"

"Ok...well technically it wasn't feeling her up because I didn't get under her clothes, but I did feel her fine boobs through her blouse and she fucking gave me a *hand job*! That's the God-honest truth! I know it sounds freakin incredible but I swear on a stack of bibles!"

"Well… okay…for the sake of conversation, let's say it really did happen like you claim it did, Marc. So she jacks you off. What happened next?"

"She even brought a hanky with her, and used it to clean the mess up afterward."

"No shit? That's pretty amazing! You think she would actually plan that? Maybe she just had the hanky with her to blow her nose or something."

While both guys digested the new information, Marc got some water at the fountain by the dugout and Robby made a quick trip to the restroom to pee.

Returning to the bleachers, Robby reviewed his take on the afternoon's activities. "Okay, so maybe you made out with this girl, and maybe felt her boobs thru her blouse. It's even possible she gave you a hand job, although it's much more likely you just came in your pants while she was rubbing you! If that's your story and you are sticking to it, okay…"

"I really haven't told you the best part yet, Robby."

"More of your fantasy BS?"

"It's *not* fantasy and *not BS*! If you don't believe me, okay, asshole, I just won't tell you the best part!"

"Okay, okay, Marc…Let's say I believe you so far. I've never known you to lie in the past. So, tell me: what's the best part?"

Somewhat mollified and dying to tell somebody about his good luck, he leaned forward and again spoke in a low voice.

"Rhonda sucked my dick clean afterward and told me in the future I can cum in her mouth, to avoid the mess!"

"No fucking way! Now you have gone too far. She actually said and did *that*? You didn't have to talk her into it? Ask her please? Beg? Plead?"

Shaking his head back and forth, Marc bragged, "Nope."

"Okay, I *really* don't believe you *now*. When Rita and I were seeing each other and we were making out, I could feel her boobs all I wanted, but if she jacked me off I had to clean it up myself. I couldn't shoot in her mouth until I told everybody she was my steady girlfriend. Even then she wouldn't swallow! Hell, that's pretty much why we're not together anymore. Rita liked me touching her but didn't really seem to like getting me off, cleaning up, or my cum."

"Well, this chick is different, and we're getting together again tomorrow. I can't wait! Blowing my load in her luscious mouth and watching her willingly swallow it will be satisfaction at its best! Fucking amazing!"

"IF all this is true, Marc, you are *one…lucky…fuck*!"

They left it at that, and both went home pondering all the amazing potentials and possibilities of a girl like Rhonda.

Pedaling home, Marc's mind was racing ahead to his next meeting with Rhonda. *Maybe I can cum on her boobs! She didn't mind when I felt them, so maybe she won't mind that, either. It'll leave a mess, though. Hopefully Rhonda will bring her hanky again next time.*

There were more questions, too. *Does bringing her hanky and possibly planning ahead mean she has done this with other guys before?* He really didn't want to ask her. It's possible she was more experienced than he was, but it really didn't matter much, anyway. *I don't really care if I am her first sexual partner or not. It actually means more to me to think Rhonda might just be showing me that she is a think-ahead, common-sense kind of girl.*

That specific hanky had been carried around in Rhonda's purse for months, just in case an opportunity like that arose, but he didn't know it.

With a big, silly grin plastered on his face, Marc considered more possibilities as he continued cycling his way home.

Maybe I could cum on her belly! A bare female belly button is very sexy.

At the beach last summer, Marc had gazed lustfully at all the tiny bikinis, letting his imagination run wild trying to visualize the secrets barely hidden beneath the tiny bits of fabric. *Roughly six to eight inches or so above those sexy belly buttons are tasty titties, and roughly six to eight inches below is tantalizing pussy. That makes a belly button an important landmark on the way to sensual pleasure and/or satisfaction either way I go!*

Ejaculating on her belly would be great because, even though it would also leave a mess temporarily, the reality of his cock being that close to her bush and boobs was definitely electrifying!

Bush - The Ultimate, Unfathomable-Yet-Incredibly-Exciting Frontier!

Until he reached that ultimate goal, however, Marc would be very glad to enjoy Rhonda's soft, warm, wet, willing, and hungry mouth…not to mention her great boobs.

His hormones running wild, Marc's thoughts leapt forward to another idea. *Maybe Rhonda can get on the Pill!* But then her parents would know she was having sex, because she was required to get their permission to get The Pill. *I would like it if she were on the Pill because it would take away the pregnancy fears for both of us; thus eliminating the main excuse she has for not allowing me to enter her. I guess a rubber will do until then.*

Marc was looking forward to tasting some boobs and pussy, however, and was pretty sure he would like it, too, but wasn't totally positive. One of the guys at school commented that not all girls' pussy tasted good but couldn't explain it any better than that. Marc didn't really know exactly what he meant. He wanted to find out for himself. *Did he mean it was sweet? Sour? Tangy? Salty? Spicy? Cherry flavored?* Nobody he knew could describe it any better, so it was just another unanswered question.

What does "ripe pussy" mean, anyway?

Chapter Eleven

As soon as Rhonda got home from the theater that Saturday afternoon, she checked in with her mom and got permission to go to Gwen's house.

Anxious to tell Gwen about every intimate detail of her inaugural experience while it was still fresh in her memory, Rhonda couldn't do it at the theater with so many people, including Alice, within earshot, so she had to contain her excitement till they got home.

Once the two friends were safely in Gwen's room with the door securely closed and locked, Rhonda described and acted out everything that had happened with Marc, going into considerable detail about her each and every sensation as it was happening.

"I was sitting on his right, like this" she said, putting herself in the role of Marc and positioning herself sitting to Gwen's left on the foot of the bed.

"Then he put his arm around my shoulders and started feeling my hair for a couple minutes. I literally got chills when he did that! Goosebumps!" Rhonda put her arm around Gwen's shoulders and ran her fingers gently along the nape of her neck and into her long, thick red hair.

"Doesn't that feel good, girlfriend?"

"Yes…it does feel nice," Gwen hesitantly replied.

After a couple minutes of this, Rhonda reported, "I didn't know what to say or do while he was doing it, so I just enjoyed it, even though it made me a little nervous and excited! Is it possible to feel too good?!"

Gwen didn't answer; she was getting a little excited and nervous, herself. *Too good?*

"Then he turned my face toward him and leaned over to kiss me, lightly at first, like this."

After Rhonda had demonstrated the kiss, Gwen admitted that kissing Marc probably felt very nice, too, just probably a little different than kissing her girlfriend. There was also an unspoken thought running through Gwen's head: *kissing Rhonda is nice, too.*

The role-playing got even more intense when Rhonda described and acted out the passionate French-kissing segment with Gwen.

Rhonda and Gwen took a break in order to collect their thoughts and composure, exactly as Rhonda had done in the theater, and for the same reason—because the passion and physical intensity were becoming overwhelming.

As long as it was Rhonda pretending to be Marc, the re-enactment wasn't as weird or awkward as it could have been. She was just acting Marc's part accurately in order to make her best girlfriend clearly understand everything exactly as it had happened.

After the French kissing resumed, Rhonda interrupted the kiss after a few minutes, as it had happened with Marc, and slowly acted out the part where his hand had trailed from her face to her neck and shoulder, and down to her breast, ending in a slow and achingly gentle and pleasurable massage.

"I almost melted into a puddle right there! It felt wonderful!" as Rhonda gently continued gently squeezing Gwen's breast. "Don't you think so too?"

Gulping hard as her brain was being flooded with warm pleasure shocks coming from her breast and spreading throughout her body, Gwen couldn't answer right away, but when she could respond, there certainly couldn't be any arguing with Rhonda's assessment.

"This Marc guy is really something if he can cause pleasures like that!" Gwen exclaimed. *Whew! Its just as good as when I stroke myself. Freakin' excellent—and I don't have to do anything!*

At each point along the way, as the role playing continued, Rhonda would look Gwen in the eye and try to read her expressions, because she didn't want to force anything on Gwen or make her uncomfortable. *This is my dearest, closest, best sweetie.*

At this point, Rhonda noticed Gwen had a sexual flush creeping up her neck and was somewhat flustered, warm, and breathing hard, too, so Rhonda halted the direct physical role play, but continued on with the descriptive details, deciding to use a prop as a visual aid instead.

Grabbing a hairbrush from the dressing table, Rhonda had Gwen hold it between her legs to simulate Marc's cock. Using the handle she demonstrated how her first real-life hard-on had been held, stroked, and kissed, finishing with an exquisitely detailed description of what it looked and felt like when Marc ejaculated.

It wasn't until Rhonda was ready to tell Gwen how the fluid smelled and tasted, that she brought out the pièce de résistance.

"Close your eyes and turn toward me, girlfriend."

Reaching into her purse Rhonda carefully removed the still-moist white handkerchief, soaked with what she liked to think of as Marc's gift, and held the sticky, rumpled mass under Gwen's nose so the male essence could be inhaled, a priceless gift from her absolute best and closest girlfriend.

Inhaling deeply, Gwen's eyes flew open. "Is that what I think it is? Is it him?" she excitedly asked.

"Yes! That, my dearest friend, is Marc's most personal and intimate masculinity, and I brought it to share with you!" Rhonda hesitated and watched Gwen's reaction before asking her next question, as the redhead seemed both intrigued and fascinated. "You wanna take a … taste too?"

"Uh…Are you kidding? I can't *wait* to smell, feel, and taste him! Did you like it, Rhonda?"

"Yes! I really liked it. Of course, it's gotten a little cold and sticky since then, but just give it a little lick."

Sticking out her tongue Gwen gently touched the tip to the hanky, which Rhonda was holding out to her as if it were her most prized possession, which it was.

Tasting and inhaling him deeply, Gwen was thrilled! *It's him! Yes! I can't believe it! Oh My God! Finally! What a thrill! So* that's *what they smell and taste like! It's like…nothing I know!*

Seeing Gwen's excited reaction, Rhonda scraped some of Marc from the hanky with her fingertip and smoothed it across her Number One' Girl's bottom lip to experience the smooth consistency and taste of him. Leaning in Rhonda immediately kissed her deeply, the masculine taste of Marc's semen seeping into each of their mouths.

It was the start of an intimate, shared, bonding moment that lasted more than ten incredible minutes, little by little, fingertip by fingertip, Gwen smoothing it on Rhonda's lips, then the favor was returned and shared in a deeply intimate kiss, until all of Marc was gone from the hanky, and transferred to the girls.

Deeply touched, the emotionally overwhelmed redhead opened her eyes, cupped Rhonda's face in her hands, and kissed her again, this time with gentle affection and gratefulness.

"That was so fucking *incredible*! Thank you *so* much! It's so…I can't…indescribably… intimate!" Moisture ran freely down Gwen's cheeks, and she was at a loss for words, temporarily. "You're…just… absolutely…the best…ever!" wrapping Rhonda in a huge heartfelt hug for ten minutes as they lay back on the bed.

The unique specialness of the shared moment was simply undeniable, to both girls. *These are two of the most exciting and satisfying experiences in my life, up until now, and they both happened on the same day, with the two people I like and care about most!* Two sexually intimate connections were made that day, one more physical and the other more emotional.

To Gwen, Rhonda's willingness to share such intimate, personal, unique secret treasure with her was a solid assurance they could, and would, truly remain Best Friends Forever. The foundation of their friendship was cemented that day with a hanky.

From then on, the special sharing of the Sexy, Soggy, Hanky became an unexpectedly meaningful ritual for the girls during each subsequent post-Marc debriefing.

Chapter Twelve

The next night after the Essex theater escapade, Rhonda and Marc met in the forest not far from their homes. On her way there, sneaking out of her house through her bedroom back door and into the streets, Rhonda quickly decided she didn't want to travel alone in the dark to meet him again. *In the future I will request, and if necessary demand, he walk me to the forest. I don't like this sneaking around and like even less being alone in the dark. I need to assert myself! I wouldn't do this for anybody else but Marc!*

Also, a pretty, young girl traveling alone at night was vulnerable; Rhonda didn't like being exposed and helpless. She also worried about being seen by a neighbor who might then tell her parents about her clandestine nighttime excursion.

Wearing her long wool coat, a long wool skirt, a long-sleeve pullover under a front-buttoned sleeveless sweater, and her knee-high boots, Rhonda dressed warm because it was a chilly night, only in the upper forties.

The more barriers the better I like it.

Spring had just begun to thaw the snow, and patches of green were sprouting up everywhere. The winter had been moderate and the daytime temperatures were in the fifties. In another month, April, it would be in the sixties during the day.

Rhonda was uncomfortable approaching the darkness of the forest because she heard owls hooting and twigs crackling as something moved through the brush. *I don't know about this. I don't like those crackling sounds at all! What if it's a bear? A mountain lion? A boar?*

Enough time had been spent at the local lake and forests with her father to know there were considerable wildlife in the area, at least a few bears and some bobcats around, let alone skunks. *I can just imagine getting sprayed by a skunk out here in the middle of the night and then trying to explain that one to my mom!*

Just then, she spotted Marc standing at the edge of the forest. *At least, I hope its Marc.* She could only see a silhouette, so far.

Whew! He's here! I don't know what I would have done if he hadn't shown up! Rhonda thought when she got close enough to make out the features of his smiling face in the faint moonlight.

With a quick kiss Marc took her hand and led her into the shadows. *Great! I was worried she would stand me up.*

A little reluctantly, Rhonda followed along. "Are you sure this is safe, Marc?"

"Sure. I come here all the time, Rhonda, and no one's ever bothered me."

"Well, have you seen any wild animals around?"

"Nope. Not once! A bunch of us guys come here sometimes to camp out overnight with a fire, and we have never had a problem, either."

"Well…I don't know…" She was not completely reassured.

Twenty steps later, he turned to her, cupped her face in his hands, and kissed her on the mouth. Her reservations about meeting him there dissolved quickly as she warmly returned his kiss.

Sliding his hands inside her coat and wrapping his strong arms around her, Marc pulled her close, merging the natural heat of their bodies together to ward off the cool night air.

Rhonda pressed herself against him, wanting to make it last, to make it a romantic, whole-body experience, not just give him a blowjob and then leave. *I want to explore him all over, kiss him everywhere, and learn about all of him and how I can please and pleasure him, starting with his mouth and his face.*

They kissed a few minutes longer, their arms tightly around one another and their tongues busily tangling.

"Do you want to sit down, Rhonda?" Marc was feeling a little warmer and weaker and was hoping maybe she might be feeling that way, too.

I can't wait to lie down with her. It's one step closer to my home-run goal.

At that point, they just agreed to sit, and then lie down on the thick bed of pine needles.

"I don't want to get my clothes dirty, Marc…or wrinkled. We need a blanket or something."

"We" …another conscious word choice of Rhonda's, just as the use of "our" had been in the theater. *One step closer to us being an actual couple, which is my eventual goal.*

A little hesitant, she lay back carefully on her long, wool coat. *In case he didn't catch my earlier hint, I'm going to ask him to bring at least one blanket next time.*

Meanwhile, Marc was thinking girls were a little silly sometimes. *Why is she so worried about a few wrinkles in her clothes? So what if she gets a little dirt smudge on her? I don't care if my clothes get wrinkled. And how dirty could we get on the three-inch thick bed of pine needles?*

But aloud all he said was: "Okay, Rhonda, I will find a blanket for next time."

Whatever I have to do to get her back to doing what we came here for...

Five more minutes of exciting mouth-to-mouth followed, and things were heating up when he rolled on top of her.

Oh, it feels good to have Marc on top of me, pressing his body against me, but he might try to go all the way with me if I let him stay there. I'm just not ready for that.

Rhonda pushed his head to the left side of her neck.

"No, not now, not yet," she murmured, turning her head slightly so her neck would be more exposed to him. *My neck is a very sensitive area and I want him to know it. I also want to distract him a bit before he gets any other wild ideas.*

"I like to be kissed there, too" she purred, indicating her neck, so he reluctantly tried it out.

Marc was confused and didn't understand what she meant. *What did she not want to do yet? I want Rhonda to know her body feels good to me. The best way to feel all of her body at once is to lie on top of her.*

Even though they were fully clothed, both realized lying together in this position was moving them further along their chosen sexual path.

Hearing her say "not yet," whatever she meant by it, was also very exciting because it meant she was agreeable to him doing more with her in the future, just not now, so Marc reluctantly decided to bide his time and started unbuttoning her sweater instead. *Should I unbutton all of the six buttons on her sweater or just enough to get my hand inside?* He wondered. *Maybe I should pull Rhonda's long-sleeved blouse out of her skirt at the waist, so I can get my hands underneath? Should I stop kissing her to unbutton her sweater and blouse?*

He decided to just unbutton her sweater the whole way but not try to take it off, especially since it was chilly out. She did not resist when Marc unbuttoned her sweater, or when he pulled her pullover out of her skirt, baring her belly and most of her chest.

Damn! It's too dark to really see anything clearly, but I can make out the outline of her bra, which seems to be kind of lacy.

Lowering his head and positioning his hand to where the cup could be pulled down just a little…

Before he could lean down to take a taste, Rhonda pulled Marc's head up and kissed him hard on the mouth, rolling on top of him simultaneously. *I'll have more control over what happens if I'm on top. He looked like he was going to put his mouth on my breast, and I'm not sure I would have been able to control myself if he had!*

Marc didn't know Rhonda was battling against her own natural urges for self-control, of course.

Pressing her breasts hard into his chest so he could feel them thru his long-sleeved jacket—but not suck them—she lunged in for a firm, passionate kiss on his mouth, eventually sliding her lips over to kiss his cheek, jaw, earlobe, and neck just below his ear. *I'm going to kiss him all over, very sensually, a little at a time. It drives me wild when Gwen does that to me! I hope it will have the same effect on him!*

At first Marc didn't know what she was doing by moving her kisses from his mouth to his face, neck, and ears, but within a few minutes he started to enjoy it. Rhonda had raised herself up to straddle him as she showered him with kisses. With her on top of him like that, her crotch was practically against his and he could only think of one thing: *how sexy it would be to have her straddling me like that if we were both naked!*

She can straddle me all she wants! Sit on me, baby! Rub that pussy all over me! Please!

While Rhonda continued to kiss him, Marc reached around under her shirt and felt for the hooks at the back of her bra.

"It hooks in the front," Rhonda whispered in his ear.

Marc muttered, "Oh, uh…thanks," because he didn't know what else to say, and brought his hands around to the front of her bra and fiddled with the clasp for a few minutes before…*Success!*

Manually massaging her boobs and playing with her large, stiff nipples is great, as she explores me with her mouth, so the pleasures were going in both directions. *Its very cool to both give and receive pleasure at the same time!*

Rhonda had considered wearing jeans, partly due to the weather but mostly due to the situation, and was glad she had at least chosen warm winter clothes. *Tight jeans next time however!*

Her skirt rode up some when she moved to straddle Marc, and he caught a view of most of her smooth, milky-white, right thigh before Rhonda quickly pulled her skirt down and adjusted her position. *Damn! I'd like to run my hands along the inside of her thigh…and get* way *closer to home!*

Catching a view up her skirt, feeling her boobs, and hearing her groan with pleasure seemed like a win-win situation to him. *It's the perfect twenty-minute sexual trifecta!*

Surprised to find several of the places she kissed him felt pretty good, sometimes very good, his friend from Down Under was awakened, causing him to strain for some attention.

I can feel his bulge growing as I sit on him. She was at least as aware of the anatomical and sexual possibilities as Marc, and probably more. *It is so close! I can almost imagine what it would feel like, but I need to control myself for now...*

Sliding up and down on his erection through his pants was a delicious, enticing idea, but she was afraid it would feel *too* good, so it was filed it away for another time, hopefully in the near future.

We are on the very same wavelength! He is this *close, inches to entering me! I wonder if Marc realizes it.*

The fact her femaleness was in such close proximity to his maleness was not lost on him at all. He almost immediately ejaculated, just considering it! *The very thought is freaking overwhelming! A matter of mere inches! Centimeters! Is she doing this to tease me? Fuck me, please! Now!*

After soaking in that sexy scenario for a full minute, Rhonda slid down his body, unbuckled his belt, unzipped his fly, reached into his underwear and withdrew her prize, marveling at the rigid miracle she had generated, again. Holding it gently in her hand, his cock flexed and pointed up to her, so she licked her lips and kissed his smiling tip. *Hello handsome! Another beautiful hard-on for me to enjoy.*

Using her hands more and kissing it occasionally for the first few moments, Rhonda then captured the tip into her mouth briefly, as a test run, to see what response she might get. Receiving a positive and pleasurable grunting and groaning response from Marc, she again supplemented her manual massage with periodic periods of oral pleasure, taking more of his member inside her lips.

I want more of him inside me!

His groans got deeper and stronger as she went deeper.

She feels fucking great! Too good? Is it possible? Damn!

His groans increased in intensity when she went further down on him, pleasing both of them but also causing her to misread his sexual signals and become afraid he was close to letting go. Sliding her lips toward the tip she licked the still-warmly-encircled slit at the tip for maybe ten seconds, without any success.

He's making sounds like he's ready to shoot!...maybe...

Sure Marc was close to releasing it, Rhonda took it out of her mouth briefly to take another deep breath, without stopping the manual massage, just as the first shot erupted.

"Oh no! I'm coming too soon! Here it comes!" It took him by surprise. He tried to resist, but it was no use.

As the first load took flight, Marc grabbed her hand and quickly moved it up and down the shaft with his for the second and third squirts, showing her the rhythm and motion required to milk him dry. Rhonda was amazed! *My eyes have grown accustomed to the dark enough to witness his sperm arcing across his belly, almost up to his chest!*

"Look out! Ohhhhh..."

Wow! I see how he likes me to move my hand, what kind of rhythm he wants and needs. She was learning fast and filed that particular hand-milking movement into her memory banks for future reference.

We did it again! Success! I'm getting good at this, leaning down to clean him up, licking first along his belly and then sucking gently on his cock, Rhonda fully enjoyed his scent and the feel of his semen on her tongue and her lips... before putting the Sexy, Soggy Hanky to work again for the final touches.

Groaning deeply once, Marc's head collapsed back onto the pine needles, eyes closed, exhausted and satisfied.

I may be a B student at school, but I feel like an Honor Roll student in Romance 101 who is learning fast and determined to be a Dean's List student in the future! Watching him spurt is like getting an A every time!

It was a close call, however, when she was straddling him. *I was* so *tempted to take him in. The* thought *of him sliding all the way inside me makes me shudder. I am* dying *to feel all of him inside me! I have to find a rubber soon—very soon!*

It was not completely clear to her whether this was really another hand job or a blow job because both her hands and her mouth were involved in his orgasm. *If its another hand job, that will be good, too, but—oh my God—if its really my first blowjob...Wow!*

The debate in her mind stopped after a couple minutes, and she decided, *either way, its great! Why over-analyze it? His shared pleasure and orgasm is the goal, and its a done deal!* Putting her head on his chest she listened to Marc's heart rate slow back to normal as his body relaxed and he nodded off to sleep. Rhonda's pulse was also slowing back to normal, along with his, and she felt very close to him then.

A relaxed and contented feeling swept over her, and she allowed herself to drift off, too, pleased with the knowledge this was the first time she ever slept with a guy, even briefly, and that magical guy was Marc.

I don't know if it's rude to go to sleep after she relaxes me, but I have absolutely no energy to talk or even move. Geez, I am surprised my heart has enough energy to continue beating. I think she's drained every molecule of energy from me!

He was more pleased, relaxed, and satisfied than ever before.

If all girls are all this much fun, my life is going to be great!

Luckily, the cold of the night roused them from their brief nap. Standing, they adjusted their clothing and brushed each other off, hoping no stray pine needles were still attached, especially to Rhonda's wool skirt and coat.

Once Marc was able to walk and talk, he explained his inability to speak afterward to her while slowly walking her back thru the forest and then the alley to her house.

"If I could talk at that point, Rhonda, I would. I just can't because I am totally exhausted. You really…uh…*drained* me!"

Insisting she understood, a part of her really did understand. *I don't want to talk much, and can't, really, right after a good, strong orgasm, either. I just want to enjoy it.* But she didn't want to share that particular bit of information with Marc.

Another part of her, however, wanted some time for snuggling together, talking, and emotional sharing, but she didn't want to spend any more time than necessary listening to the owls hoot and the twigs snapping in the darkness. *Besides, I don't want to stay out so long my parents might find out I'm not in my room.*

Rhonda later voiced her satisfaction, tinged with disappointment, to Gwen. "I'm fine with all of the sexy physical stuff; it's awesome! But I also want to feel close to Marc. I want him to talk with me, tell me how he feels about me, and let me know who he really is. You know, some emotional bonding to complete the experience. Do you think that's possible with a guy?"

After a couple long, intimate discussions with Gwen, it was decided maybe Marc, like a lot of guys, just didn't know how to express his feelings. It was agreed Rhonda should start showing him, leading by example. *Expressing some of my feelings for him will be pretty easy for me.*

Chapter Thirteen

The next day Rhonda didn't see Marc at all at school. However, they had agreed the night before to meet later that evening for another exciting jaunt into the woods.

Since Rhonda had been uncomfortable sneaking through the streets alone at night, when she mentioned it to him walking back to her house, Marc gladly agreed to meet her at the back gate in the dark alley behind her house. A thick, six-foot-high hedge all around Rhonda's back yard shut out nearly all the surrounding light, except from the security light directly over the back gate, so it was a good place for them to meet and not readily be seen.

Seeing him at the back gate at 8:30 that Sunday night was exciting, and got even better as he escorted her to the forest, carrying a small, white blanket for them to lie on, pleasing both of them.

I like lying down with her, in general, because it's another step toward real sex, and don't want her wrinkled or possibly dirty clothes to be an issue standing in our way.

To Rhonda, the blanket lessened the chance of her clothes getting dirty or having pine needles stick to them. *It also will help keep us a bit warmer.*

She also appreciated that Marc had actually granted her very reasonable request for a blanket, and for him to escort her to and from the forest. *It also gives me the feeling of being a liberated woman because I successfully took some control of the situation and my own safety and well-being. I have asserted myself!*

Not wanting him to be getting too many sexy ideas, though, while they were again lying on the forest floor, Rhonda took control and quickly rolled on top of him while they were kissing. Wanting it to last longer and to enjoy all of him, she began pressing her soft mouth to his face and ears, putting her tongue in his ear and brushing her lips along his neck as his jacket was pulled open and shirt unbuttoned.

Slowly working her way south, kissing his bare chest and belly, Rhonda enjoyed making him groan as she went along. *I've fantasized about this so many times, and now I'm actually doing it!*

Staying true to the plan she and Gwen had devised, Rhonda began throwing out some simple, expressive statements and questions.

"I like kissing your chest. Do you like it too?"

"Uh huh…"

The few sprigs of hair on his chest tickled her lips and her nose.

"Does this feel good, Marc, or do you like it more this way?" moving her lips one way, and then another.

"Uh huh… yeah… nice…"

Marc was completely clueless as to how he should respond when Rhonda said those kinds of things to him and asked him stuff. *What should I say? 'Yes,' 'no,' and 'thank you' don't seem to satisfy her. She seems like she's waiting for me to say more. What in the world could she want?*

Rhonda wasn't completely happy with his brief, undetailed responses, but at least he uttered a few words. *Grunts and one-word verbal cues will have to do for now, I guess.* Those areas eliciting a moan, grunt, or groan were mentally filed away so they could be returned to quickly in the future, or whenever she wanted.

A certain spot on his chest made him moan. *I can tell he also really enjoys when I put my tongue in his ear, rub my breasts all over his chest and belly, and continue my kisses, caresses, and strokes in a slowly southerly direction. His cock gives him away.*

Unbuttoning her blouse while in a lip lock Marc was very happy to find another front-hook bra, which made it easy for him. He was amazed when her beautiful breasts appeared this time with only a little shyness and reticence on her part. "Your boobs are so soft and warm!"

I'm not sure if she will mind me referring to her breasts as boobs, or not. Maybe Rhonda likes the term "titties" better.

When she just smiled, he was relieved.

"I like your big stiff nipples too!" he followed up quickly.

She was pleased to receive the compliment. "I like the way you touch my breasts and massage them. Don't be afraid to squeeze them some, too. It feels so good!"

I know she refers to her boobs as "breasts," but that doesn't sound as sexy or fun to me as "boobs" or "titties."

Heeding her request, Marc kneaded her breasts, watch her kiss and lick his belly while rubbing and squeezing his now-erect cock through his jeans. Firmly pinching her stiff nipples, she closed her eyes and groaned. Not knowing if he had

74

squeezed too hard or not, and not wanting to hurt her, Marc stopped.

Five seconds later Rhonda opened her eyes. "Why did you stop? That felt really nice!"

Firm nipple pinching and plucking was willingly and gladly resumed, now he knew she liked it. *I'm enjoying making her groan with pleasure, too.*

Rhonda's focus was now a search for those other spots that pleased him. *While I am looking forward to having Marc explore my body the same way, its much safer for me to explore him for now.* She didn't want things to progress more quickly than her self-control could handle.

I'd better not rub my breasts too high on Marc's chest because he might take a quick taste—a taste I will like way *too much!*

Marc was surprised at how much he liked having Rhonda kiss him all over. *No one's ever done that to me, before. I wonder how she knows to do it. God, I really like when she sticks her tongue in my ear. It's sexy as hell!*

"That feels nice, Rhonda. Your tongue tickles some, but it feels good, too." he hesitantly stated, responding verbally to her kisses, finally, and causing her to smile.

Progress.

Although he didn't know exactly what to stay, Marc was smart enough to realize that he could, and should, start giving Rhonda the personal and sexual compliments she deserved. Otherwise, her feelings might change towards him and the making out and his oh-so-satisfying ejaculations with her could come to a screeching halt.

Kissing and exploring Rhonda all over had occurred to Marc early on, but he hadn't really thought about the possibility of her having those same ideas about him until she was actually already doing it.

Marc didn't know exactly what Rhonda was doing or why, but it felt good, even if it wasn't overtly sexual. *My jaw aches from wanting to taste her titties,* but she just continued her pleasurable explorations of him, keeping herself just out of titty-tasting range, so he closed his eyes and relaxed. Pleased but a little frustrated, and not so perfectly patient, he pleasurably bided his time.

"Do you want me to kiss you all over, too?" he asked her, ever hopeful.

"Not yet," she replied. "I'm enjoying exploring *you* right now," she added with a sly little smirk. "Do you like it too? Seems like I've hit a couple good spots so far, right"

Marc just nodded. He was still thinking about her words: "Not yet," was a good sign to Marc. *She's seriously considering it!*

Rhonda was pleasantly surprised and pleased to find she also liked kissing his body everywhere, making him groan, and hearing him respond to her touches, strokes, caresses, and kisses. To her, it was another way she could extend their frankly explicit carnal meetings into full romantic experiences.

She tried to creatively think of what to do next. *I would lick his nipples, but he might like it too much and want to lick mine, too! I'll just rub my nipples on his, instead, and see how he likes that.*

The full-body exploration concept had actually originated in a steamy romance novel Rhonda had recently found hidden away in her mom's bedroom closet. She and Gwen had read it several times at length in secret on sleepovers late into the night

76

and discussed it in detail. They had also acted it out on each other, so this was not really Rhonda's first experience with this kind of exploratory endeavor. *This is a chance, however, to actually do it with a guy! It's another page in my education about guys, sex, and romance.*

With each new experience, Rhonda's confidence in her prowess as a lover grew, thoroughly enjoying her newfound ability to make Marc groan at will. *I don't know if he minds me undressing him in the forest or not, but I'm going to be topless soon, so it's only fair if he's partially undressed, too. What's good for the goose is good for the gander! Equal opportunities!*

Trailing her fingers along the inside of his waistband, Rhonda gave him a quick look to see his response, but Marc's eyes were closed and he made no gestures of protest, resistance, or shyness, just groans of pleasure, so her sensual explorations continued uninterrupted.

As it had been rehearsed dozens of times in her past fantasies, she unbuckled his belt, unbuttoned the waist at the top of his jeans, and unzipped his fly. Her hands trembling with excitement rather than nervousness, Rhonda pulled down his white Jockey underwear enough to touch his soft, curly pubic hair, noticing it was much like her own. *I like running my fingers through it while nuzzling his cock with the tip of my nose, again breathing him in deeply.* She couldn't wait to tell Gwen what it was like to undress Marc, to see and feel his private, hidden areas in the shadows and dim, moonlit night.

Adding to the excitement, Marc is undressing me at the same time! He wants to undress me! Does he like what he sees and feels? Am I attractive to him? Maybe even sexy?

Apparently yes, but he never exactly verbalized those words. *I wish he would tell me more. I want to hear him say he likes me, likes kissing me, and likes touching me.*

As she pulled his jeans and underwear down past his knees to his ankles, she felt a sense of power. *Liberated ladies take control! In my imagination I am also liberating his cock, too!* A powerful hard-on greeted her with a big smile!

There you are again! Hello, handsome! Giving it a kiss.

Now wanting her to see and know how excited he was to be with her, Marc thought his ramrod hard-on would make it crystal clear.

There's no doubt I am glad to see that his Friend from Down Under is also glad to see me! Another fabulous hard-on to my credit! What a beautiful thing we have again created together.

With his underwear completely out of the way this time, Rhonda had full access to Marc's other male attribute she was curious about: his balls. *I am glad they aren't hidden this time. In the theater I was only able to pull only his cock through the little front opening in his briefs.*

Once his pants were down, Rhonda moved to his left side so he could massage her breasts easier while ministering to him.

"Let me shift…over here…it'll be better for both of us."

Glancing over, Marc tucked Rhonda's blouse back a bit so he could have a better view of her breasts. He thought of the two *Playboy* magazines, loaned to him by a baseball buddy, currently hidden under his mattress and brought out at night as inspiration. Compared to the *Playboy* pictures of Playmate breasts he and his buddies ogled and drooled over for hours, Rhonda's appeared to be very similar.

Reaching over, he happily resumed fondling them.

Wrapping her hand around the base of his length, Rhonda licked the beautiful, soft tip twice and captured him in soft, warm, oral sexiness. *It took him a few minutes to shoot his load before at the movies, and a little less time last night. With any luck at all, I am again going to set your cock and cum free tonight, cowboy!*

"Jesus! This feels freakin' great! I could enjoy an hour of this! Maybe two hours! Don't stop!" Mark told her as the pleasures quickly multiplied.

Oh no! It feels too *good! I can't stop it! Oh nooo...!*

Rhonda was very surprised when, in less than a minute of soft sexy sweet suckling, a semen-shot bounced off the back of her throat.

Shit! I'm coming too soon! Waaay *too soon! Fuck me!*

Rhonda struggled to continue milking Marc with her hand while coughing and gagging. *Whoops! Oh no...!*

The first spurt stimulated her gag reflex, causing her to cough it onto his belly as she removed it from her mouth, hacking. The second shot sprayed across her nose onto her forehead. The third shot splattered across her cheek and chin.

Christ! She's really gonna be pissed. What a mess!

Rhonda couldn't fully enjoy his spasms because she was coughing and gagging from the first shot. *It was so fast, I wasn't ready for it! I wish I could have stopped and gotten a breath. I could have kept him going with my hand and still swallowed some. Once he starts into his orgasm, there's no stopping it until it's finished, just like mine. His cock and cum are liberated, it's true, but not like I originally planned!*

Another lesson was learned the hard way, and it was a mess.

Marc simply couldn't help it. *The pleasure of her incredible mouth wrapping around me, of her kissing and caressing me, is freaking indescribable!* Besides the obvious physical pleasure her velvet lips provided, the visual stimulation of watching her gladly and willingly take his cock into her mouth was too much to resist. *I am defenseless! Rhonda Bell is actually sucking my cock! Yes! Hell yes! Willingly! Damn! Fuck yeah! It's happening! A* diatribe ran unbidden through his mind as he had watched her give him his—and her—first un-freaking-believable blow job.

*Jesus H. Christ! Did **that** feel good!!!! Hand jobs are good, but blow jobs are even better! WAY better!*

On his way to the forest, Marc had anticipated and looked forward to enjoying her enticing sexy mouth, which turned him on considerably, and now it had happened! He wanted it to continue for a long time, but simply couldn't control himself. *Rhonda wants me inside her, at least in her mouth. It's a start!*

His curiosity about girls and the pleasure and satisfaction they can provide was being answered.

When he recovered, Marc apologized, but Rhonda didn't seem very disturbed. *I hope she isn't too pissed off by my shooting too quickly!*

"Sorry...I just couldn't hold it anymore! It felt *so* freakin' good!"

He also apologized for ejaculating in her throat and causing her to gag, making a mess. *I wanted to shoot my load in her mouth all along, so the apology isn't for that, but I really do feel bad about shooting so early and making her cough and gag.*

She insisted it was all right, but he wasn't so sure. *I certainly wouldn't like someone making a mess all over me! Maybe a faceful of pussy juice would be okay, though!*

He tried to explain that it simply felt too good to resist, but wasn't sure if she heard him or not. There was only an awareness of his own immense pleasure and satisfaction, of the sensual tsunami overcoming him and carrying him over the cliff, and Marc had no idea she enjoyed his orgasm too, even though it *did* make a considerable mess.

In reality, I enjoyed myself immensely for the entire minute before it abruptly ended, and I was mildly disappointed Marc stopped massaging my breasts once he came. But overall, she considered it to be a very successful outing. *I did it again! My first real, official blowjob! Licking the tip next time will be better, I think. Coughing and sputtering around was really embarrassing!*

After she licked the semen off his belly they both scraped the fluid from her face with their forefingers and put it in her waiting open mouth. In Rhonda's mind, they were working together as a team—or even a *couple*.

When most of the mess was gone, she took her handkerchief out of her purse and proceeded to gently clean what remained. The Sexy, Soggy Handkerchief gladly came to the rescue again, pleasing both of them, for different reasons.

The bottom line is, all of his sperm is mine and mine alone. Rhonda decided she would take his gift in almost any manner Marc wanted to give it, but he didn't know it, and she wasn't ready for him to know it, yet.

"Let me get that, Rhonda," Marc offered, scraping some of the sticky stuff from her chin. "Sorry…"

Marc saying my name while scooping his fluid into my mouth with his own finger pleases me. To her, it was an intimate, caring act. *He obviously wants me to have it all, and I obviously want every drop! And I love to hear him say my name.*

To Marc, it was simply good manners. *I have made a huge mess, so I'd better help her clean it up.*

Soon, Rhonda's glow of satisfaction faded slightly as questions began running through her mind. *Is having his sperm all over my face a turn-on to him, or a turn-off? Would it be a disappointment after I promised to swallow it all in the future? Was it my fault he ejaculated so soon? Maybe it was his fault, or maybe we are both at fault.*

She'd coughed the first spurt back onto his belly, which had added to the mess, but he didn't mention it at all. *Is he angry? Disappointed? Does his semen all over my face make me ugly or unattractive to him? Maybe it makes me prettier to him because it's his semen. Do I dare ask him?*

It was hard to tell from his reaction. It wasn't clear if he considered her face pretty or not, with or without the splattered semen, as he never voiced his opinion about it at all. *I hope Marc thinks I am pretty, and assume since we are together, he does, but I still want to hear him say something nice, any kind of compliment will be welcome.*

When he apologized profusely and helped her wipe some of it off her face, Rhonda realized it wasn't anybody's fault. *It's just something unexpected. Having Marc apologize is a sign he is taking some of the sexual responsibility, too, which is good.* At that point, Rhonda decided it wasn't necessarily a bad thing for either one of them.

Marc is obviously satisfied, which was my intent all along. It just happened before either one of us wanted it to happen. It was unfortunate timing. Next time, the timing will be better. I'll take my time because I really do like spending time with him. Just being with him makes my day!

Rhonda eventually decided that because she was so excited to suckle his beautiful cock again, he was overwhelmed with too much pleasure too quickly. *What a lovely thought! I sucked him too well, too fast, flooding him with pleasurable sensations. I will pace myself better next time and we'll both enjoy it longer.*

From the experience, Rhonda learned she could cause him to ejaculate quickly, very quickly, intentionally or unintentionally. Also, she would have to take her time in the future so the delightful breast massage would last longer. Once Marc had ejaculated, he obviously stopped paying attention to her for a while afterward. *Both are good lessons to learn! Its particularly pleasing for me to think I suckled him **too** good! Next time I'll use my tongue-deflector.*

However, Rhonda didn't know Marc had been very excited in anticipation of the rendezvous himself, before she even arrived, so the quick ejaculation was really due to a combination of factors.

"Is there any still on my face or in my hair, Marc?" *I love saying his name as much as I love hearing him say mine.*

Marc would never know it, but Rhonda actually liked seeing his seminal fluid spurt in her direction. The visual delight she took in it was in addition to all of the overt pleasures derived from it just *being* Marc. In addition, it left proof on the Sexy, Soggy Hanky to share with Gwen afterward.

The physical remains of his experience with her would be discussed, dissected, tasted, inhaled deeply, shared and thoroughly enjoyed by the two girls, but he had no clue it was happening, and they had no intention of telling him.

From Marc's perspective, the hanky was just very practical.

Another thing I won't tell him is how having his sperm sprayed all over my face actually pleases me! Facials will be allowed, and even privately enjoyed, as long as there is little or no chance of being discovered by others. She certainly didn't want her parents or anyone else to question her about the soon-to-be dried, flaky goop all over her face!

Otherwise I'll just quickly swallow it, which eliminates the evidence and makes me feel good because I have something very precious of Marc's inside of me. That makes me feel special, like he's chosen me, and only me, to receive his gift.

Marc, of course, did not know Rhonda was looking at his ejaculation as a gift for her. The very idea and concept that a female might allow him to ejaculate in her face, much less enjoy it, was both exciting and bewildering to Marc. *What possible pleasure could there be for her? It's the same with blow jobs. It's obvious why I like it, but what could she possibly get out of it?*

Mind you, he wasn't going to try to dissuade her in the least because there was another strong biological part of him that was screaming for her to do exactly that! *Not only do I want her to take it in but its also important Rhonda absorb me in the sexy and friendly pleasing manner in which I give it to her!*

Chapter Fourteen

Continuing their forest outings over the next week or so, Rhonda experimented with ways to make their experience last longer. One way was to keep Marc on his feet, at first, while she got on her knees and began to suckle him. *I want to see how long he can last before letting it go,* she thought.

Marc seemed to like the new stance, too. "God yes! That feels great! Lick it! Kiss it some more, up and down, top and bottom, Rhonda!"

I really like to please him and hear him groan my name.

After ten minutes, he was practically begging for relief and release, needing to lie down, but she was enjoying herself a lot and wanted to test her, and Marc's, sexual limits.

Just like Rhonda, he wanted the entire experience to last longer, and now it was.

When he got close to letting go, Marc would warn her about the impending discharge and lie down to finish.

"I better lie down now, Rhonda, before I fall down! Oh! God! Yes! Here it comes! Look out!"

Even though his spasm was hard and strong, Rhonda didn't flinch an inch, slurping him up and downing him in one smooth motion and three seriously satisfying swallows.

Damn! That feels so freaking great! Again! YES-s-s-s!...

Marc was truly enjoying himself, yet, at the same time, he wanted to try some more things on Rhonda. *She still won't let me kiss or suck her titties, though, and is resistant to anything more than what we are already doing.*

Hearing her groan and seeing her with her eyes closed and thrusting her hips forward and back as he touched her breasts, was a new and exciting experience for him. *I can please and pleasure her too! Apparently her titties and her hips, maybe even her pussy, are connected, somehow!*

Another new thing Rhonda tried with Marc was rubbing her boobs on his cock. *I can have him sit on my chest so I can capture his cock between my breasts and feel him pushing forward and back between them. When I take his tip in my mouth as he pushes forward, it's like he is thrusting inside me!* She thought with an unrequited whimper and groan.

Titty fucking was one step closer to the eventual goal for them both.

All the while, Rhonda was actually stalling for time, exploring a wide variety of safe and satisfying sexual alternatives while searching desperately for a rubber, which would safely allow them to do what they both really wanted: full penetration with excellent protection.

It would finally be *making love,* to Rhonda.

From Marc's perspective, *it will be a very friendly, fun, sensual, safe, and satisfying loss of virginity—for both of us.*

Chapter Fifteen

Marc was desperately trying to find a rubber too, for the same reasons as Rhonda, but also without any luck. *I don't know who to ask, where to get one, what brand or size, and am as uninformed as she probably is, probably more, about rubbers.*

They met every day or every other day or so for some form of oral sex and titty play for that week. Marc usually called her or talked with her briefly in the hall at school to arrange further sexual rendezvous, getting quickly to the point without much chit chat or personal interaction.

As a result of our frequent meetings, I stopped pleasuring myself on a daily basis and leave it up to Rhonda to pleasure and relieve me most days, because she's so much better at it.

Marc sometimes relieved himself at home thinking about her on her knees, topless, and draining him, because it was a very sexy visual, but quickly decided it was better to wait for her sexiness, as the orgasm Rhonda provided was *much* more pleasurable and required absolutely *no* effort on his part.

If a day was missed, by the second day he was pretty horny, his surge was strong, and he would often ejaculate twice in less than a half hour. Rhonda was pleasantly surprised to learn Marc could have two orgasms so close together, but glad to be of service. *It allows me to spend more quality time with him after the initial series of spurts.*

After his initial ejaculation, Marc thoroughly enjoyed himself, mostly reveling in the simple, uncomplicated pleasure and satisfaction of his orgasm, at that point, and looking forward to his next hard-on and oh-so-pleasant release.

Ejaculating twice with Rhonda in thirty or forty minutes pleased her because it was a pretty good indicator no other girl had received his cum in the meantime. *Marc is saving it for me, (*which he was*), and the thought alone pleases me greatly.*

The only troubling part was, after his load was deposited in her mouth or her face, he wouldn't kiss her again.

In his mind, it was strange or even gay for him to possibly get some semen in his mouth, even if Rhonda insisted she had swallowed it all. *What if she still has cum on her tongue, or on her lips? Only gay guys taste semen! My interest is in tasting pussy, not sperm!*

Reproduction, romance, or even relationships weren't anywhere on his near-term or long-term radar. His lower brain was pretty much in charge.

Chapter Sixteen

After the first week of their sexual rendezvous, Rhonda wanted Marc to tell everyone at school she was his girlfriend, but he insisted there was no time in his busy school/sports schedule for a steady girlfriend.

I won't push him too hard because I like him, am really enjoying him, and learning a lot. I'll wait a month and ask him again, if he hasn't asked me already.

Rhonda considered Marc to be her first real boyfriend even though he really didn't think of her as a girlfriend. To him, a girlfriend was someone to be courted, wooed, and shown off. *I mostly consider Rhonda to be a nice, horny, curious younger girl with a nice body who willingly gives excellent head and definitely has further sexual potential.*

From his perspective, she wanted to learn how to make out and suck cock and Marc was very happy to help Rhonda in her educational efforts because he, too, was amazingly horny and curious. *She's a fast learner and a sexy, willing partner, and I like that about her. I'm also willing to help her out when she is ready for screwing, and as horny as she is, it won't be very long. I hope not! The sooner the better!*

Realizing that even nice girls got horny and wanted sex was an awakening to Marc. *Sex isn't something guys do to girls, it is something guys do* with *girls. It's a cooperative effort, not necessarily a seduction, rape, or a power struggle like some of the radical feminists say. We are in it together, literally.*

Once Marc got into Rhonda's pants he would probably have to publicly announce her as his girlfriend, limiting his sexual opportunities with other girls but insuring his near-term sexual future.

Like a lot of young guys his age, his thinking was basically all about getting off. *She's a nice girl who provides me a lot of fun, pleasure, and satisfaction, but there are lots of other nice girls out there to be explored and enjoyed.*

Rhonda's age also had something to do with his reluctance to acknowledge her as his steady girlfriend. *If Rhonda were in my grade I would probably tell everyone she was my girlfriend. But I don't want to get razzed by the other guys for dating jailbait, robbing the cradle, and generally not being able to get a girl my own age. Shoot, I've done some of that razzing myself, and I don't want the aggravation.*

An undercover affair is the perfect answer - all the benefits and none of the drawbacks. And it doesn't limit my sexual chances with other females.

Chapter Seventeen

After their fifth meeting in the woods, Rhonda began inviting Marc over to her house while her parents went out to eat dinner, dance, and have a few drinks at the Country Club, three or four times a week. (Her dad's business associates met there, and they always talked some business so they could deduct the evening expenses from their taxes.) *My house is comfortable, clean, and warm, and there are no disturbing forest noises in the background.*

Knowing approximately what time her parents came home after the Club, usually 10:30 or so, and that her little sister was usually studying at the library with Gwen's little sister most nights until Shirley brought the girls home when it closed at 10pm, made her projections easier. *I can plan pretty accurately our agenda and what time I have to have Marc safely out of the house.*

Rhonda insisted right from the first visit to her house Marc know the emergency plan, in case her parents returned early. Luckily, she lived in a one-story house, so it wouldn't be too hard for Marc to get out through the back door in a hurry. The house actually had three back doors: one, a sliding glass door, led from the dining room onto the jalousie Florida room; the other was a standard back door exiting directly from the kitchen to the back yard, plus the exit out of her bedroom. The kitchen door was the one she instructed him to use.

"Here's the kitchen, and the back door leads thru the back yard to the alley. See the light, Marc?" opening the back door so he could see the gate where they had met when they walked together to the forest. Marc nodded.

"If we see headlights pulling into the driveway early, you'll have to leave thru the back door— fast."

"Okay." It made perfect sense, and Marc was anxious to get started, so he quickly agreed. *I'm glad she's thinking ahead. I sure don't want to get caught with my pants down in her parent's home!*

Hoping she would lead him right to her bedroom, he was a little disappointed when she smiled, took his hand, and led him to the sofa next to the front door, instead. His mild discontent passed quickly passed when Rhonda sat down next to him, turned to cup his face in her hands, and gently kissed him on the mouth. *This is a pretty good start and hopefully things will get even better from here!*

The only worrisome problem with the emergency plan was, to her, Marc's typical inability to walk, let alone run, for about fifteen minutes after ejaculation. *If my parents come during that time frame, we might be screwed.*

It was definitely a risk worth taking, however.

Earlier that day, Rhonda had confided her plans to Gwen.

"If he rings my doorbell at eight, Marc should be fully recovered and gone by the time my parents return around ten thirty. Nobody will know anything. It will also give me some time to share the experience and The Sexy, Soggy Hanky with you in my bedroom, afterward." Everything was falling into place.

Each time Marc came over, their activities pretty much followed the same pattern.

Rhonda and Marc would go right to making out on the sofa, and he would unbutton her blouse to get to the front-hook bra she always wore, making it easy to bare her breasts.

Pulling Marc's pants and underwear down to his ankles, or sometimes all the way off, was something she totally enjoyed, although never knowing exactly when her parents were coming home made the ankles a better and quicker choice, and easier to pull back up should her parents surprise them.

Their making out and undressing usually took about ten to fifteen minutes and the manual and/or oral massage another ten minutes or so until Marc would reach his point of no return.

In the comfort of her home, Rhonda could relax, and quickly realized she possessed a natural talent for sucking cock. "His cock is a perfect fit for my mouth, Gwen," she confessed after a particularly arousing episode with Marc one evening. "I wanted to take all of it in my mouth at one time, because it *is* my ultimate goal to have all of him inside me, but I couldn't do it without gagging. I tried. I can't wait for the day when I can actually feel all of him inside me—no gagging, just pure joyous pleasure!"

Deep inside Rhonda knew Marc would be a perfect romantic fit when the lovemaking opportunity presented itself. "The very *thought* of him inside me is simply electrifying, Gwen!"

Her horny neighbor smiled deliciously at that very intimate thought. "God, I want a guy like Marc too."

To her surprise Rhonda found she could actually satisfy Marc to completion in about a minute if her mouth and hands were used together just right.

93

But since Rhonda's goal was more time with him, not less, she mentally filed her newfound skill, a quickie, away for future enjoyment.

Marc wanted to prolong the pleasuring process, too, so he tried to hold off a little while whenever possible. Once, he even tried thinking of his favorite major leaguer's lifetime batting averages to distract himself from the growing pleasures, but it didn't help him last any longer. It soon became clear Rhonda could make him ejaculate almost any time she wanted—thirty seconds, five minutes, ten minutes, it didn't matter.

She is in charge.

As time went on, Rhonda began altering her approach, still holding his cock with her hand at the base but with more kisses and licks and less sucking until she was ready for him to let it loose.

Licking the tip avoided any more choking, like the other girls had warned previously, and Rhonda found a quick-and-clean swallow came naturally to her. *I love the wet and warm spurts in my mouth and the smell and taste of Marc afterward on my lips.*

She explained to Gwen one day, "I love sucking it dry and getting those last remaining drops, Gwen, but when all of him is inside me there isn't much leftover for the Sexy, Soggy, Hanky!"

With experimentation, Rhonda found once the main three thrusts were done, she could milk the last few emissions with her hand and put the tip on her upper lips so she could smell him and there would be some oozing left to wipe off with her favorite cleanup/sharing device.

Marc was amazed and very pleased with her sexual abilities. *I wonder if all girls can do the same thing!? It's the best feeling I have ever known! How could she ever feel any better?*

94

Wrapping his mind around the possibility females could actually enjoy sucking him off and swallowing it was still difficult for Marc. There wasn't any use arguing with the facts because Rhonda showed him different, but he couldn't fathom the possible pleasure there might be in it for her. *All I know is that I enjoy it and it feels awesome.* That much was easy for him to understand.

Rhonda not only liked having him in her mouth, she actually liked being in the different positions to do it. When she was on her knees if front of him, Rhonda felt somehow naturally sexy and empowered.

"You know, it might sound weird, Gwen, but I *like* being on my knees in front of him. There is just something so… sexy?… about it. It feels natural, normal…submissive? The very *thought* of submitting to him turns me on! That might not sound very liberated, but it is *my choice* to be there!? Liberation is about making one's own choices. But really, even though I'm on my knees in front of him, I feel the power is mine to buckle his knees and take every ounce of energy and passion from him whenever I want. How cool is that? I am truly calling the shots, from my knees!"

It was quite an awakening for all three of them, in a way.

The ability to overcome Marc's desires was hers, if she wanted it. Fortunately for both of them, Rhonda wanted to make it last as long as possible, too.

Playing with her very nice boobs added to his and her intense pleasure. *I really enjoy being able to please her for myself, as a guy who can please a girl, but also because the more I massage, squeeze, and pluck her boobs and nipples, the more she is turned on, which leads to her sucking, kissing, and licking me even better. The more excited she is, the closer I am to exploring, pleasing, and enjoying the rest of her. Her ass starts moving, too!*

Rhonda's hip movements and increased excitement also got Marc thinking about a couple other things: *one, are her boobs and her hips connected somehow? And two, he wondered if she'd had an orgasm while sucking his cock. How will I know if she comes, too? Will she tell me? My orgasm is very obvious, but what about hers? Is it possible? Should I ask her? Could she have an orgasm from me playing with her fine titties? Is her orgasm different than mine?*

Rhonda thoroughly enjoyed pleasuring him to completion, but also enjoyed him manually massaging her breasts and plucking her nipples, so she learned to dial back her sexual intensity inside herself, and toward Marc, providing both a satisfying experience.

Without discussion they decided, over time, the entire satisfying experience would consist of a few minutes of making out, about twice that long for them to pleasure each other, to his eventual completion, and then still have enough time for him to recover before he had to leave.

Rhonda viewed Marc's recovery period as her opportunity to snuggle with him, even though he was usually too exhausted to talk much, if at all.

"I like lying next to him, topless, my head on his chest or belly, listening to his heart rate slow down and relax, knowing he is totally and completely relaxed and satisfied and his heart is so close to mine, with the proof safely inside me—and all the credit is mine, Gwen."

"It sounds very pleasurable and fulfilling, Rhonda, to both of you. I can't wait to do it myself!"

"Sometimes, though, I get so turned on doing him, especially when he's touching me, that I almost orgasm, myself, and I don't want to do that with him, yet. God, Gwen! I love his cock! I love kissing it, tasting it, and making it squirt!"

It was then Rhonda also admitted there were warm and special feelings for Marc, too, and not just lust. "I think I love him, Gwen. I'm not really positive because he's my first real boyfriend, but I get butterflies in my stomach and my heart races when I get a glimpse of him in the halls, hear his voice, or think about meeting him again."

Rhonda would never have been accused of studying too much, just enough to get mostly B's and a few A's and keep her parents happy, but since Marc entered her life her mind was mainly focused on him—processing thoughts and feelings, making plans, and sharing it all with Gwen. School became an occasional afterthought, and mainly an opportunity to see him again, talk to him, and hear his voice, in public.

In addition, she'd almost stopped fantasizing about all the other guys, including the good-looking actors and famous rock musicians who used to turn her on. Rhonda liked staying home at night, now, hoping Marc would call, thinking about him and the future. *It has become almost impossible to think about anything or anybody else. He's even invaded my dreams!*

As much as Rhonda loved sharing with Gwen, there were times she wanted to be alone, to think about *him*. As soon as Rhonda entered her house from the forest, while the memory was fresh in her mind, she did a detailed and very satisfying mental and manual replay to completion in her bed or the shower. *Its for me and Marc only, not to be shared with anybody, not even Gwen, yet.*

Once her orgasmic glow subsided, she would make a call next door to come over so they could share each and every detail, which was a priceless experience for them both that further strengthened their already-close bond.

Pulling Rhonda out of her reverie, Gwen said, "Well, if you love him, why don't you let yourself go a little and just cum with him?"

"First of all, I'm not ready for him to see me having an orgasm. I don't want him to know I'm enjoying it so much. If I get in the throes of an orgasm, my defenses would be down, and God only knows what would happen next! I don't want to take the chance of going all the way until we're both completely protected! Second, I'm afraid I might *bite* him if I orgasm when he's in my mouth. Besides, I want him to think I'm doing it for him, not me."

"Oh, okay. I guess that all makes sense. The last thing you want to do is get pregnant!"

"That's for sure. The Pill will allow me to decide when I get pregnant. I want to have a career, see the world, and live my life the way I desire. If I were eighteen, I'd just get on the Pill, but for now I'd be happy to find a rubber. Anyway, I just don't want Marc to know he can pleasure me that much, yet. It's my secret, for now."

For those reasons, Rhonda dialed back her pleasure purposefully and intentionally while actively pleasing him, letting herself go closer and closer to orgasm at times as the breast massage and nipple pulling, pinching, and plucking pleasures mounted, and then reluctantly but necessarily backing away just before reaching her point of no return, forward and back, forward and back, as she was pleasing him.

From Rhonda's cues, Marc discovered she got particularly excited when her nipples were squeezed hard, plucked repeatedly and firmly, and twirled between his thumb and forefinger. *I like making her groan, too, and playing with her titties makes both of us groan! Somehow, it also makes her butt twitch!*

98

Marc didn't know it, but part of Rhonda was dying for him to lick, kiss, and suckle her nipples, but she knew if it happened there would be no resolve left in her to resist his, and her, ultimate sexual urges.

"I just know if he kisses my breasts I am as good as screwed, Gwen!" she helplessly admitted one night when reviewing the latest visit. "I just love it! I admit it. If anybody knows how much I love it, it's you!"

Rhonda knew just the smooching and breast massages sent several electrical shocks coursing throughout her chest, down and across her abdomen, sinking deliciously lower thru her pelvis, making a warm and sweet juiciness, melting, and wanting deep inside her, but Marc didn't have a clue anything that exciting was percolating, and she had no intention of telling him.

Marc will find out his effects on me when I'm ready.

As long as he didn't know the physical and emotional pleasure his breast massages brought to her loins, she was in control, and Rhonda truly enjoyed being in control.

My orgasm will follow within a minute after he leaves my house, requiring little manual massage to make it happen, just a slow-motion, eyes closed, mental replay of the previous thirty minutes or so and a digital twitch or two. She was already close when he left, but Marc had no clue, and Rhonda wanted to keep that secret to herself!

It is, however, a delicious and sensual secret I readily and gladly share with Gwen, to our mutual delight.

Chapter Eighteen

With Gwen, Rhonda did not feel the need to hold back. There was no fear of pregnancy or disease with her, and there was already a high level of trust and intimacy. As Rhonda's and Marc's experimentation increased, so did Rhonda's and Gwen's.

In the beginning, it was primarily role playing, with either Rhonda or Gwen playing the part of Marc. When it was Gwen's turn to take on his role, Rhonda would coach her as to exactly how Marc kissed her—how hard or soft, for how long, with tongue or not—how it felt when he put his tongue in her ear, and how slow or fast he undressed her and caressed her breasts.

Being a very curious and horny student, Gwen followed Rhonda's directions well, plus she had some additional sexy ideas of her own. For example, *it was my sweetie who taught me how sensitive, sexy, and kissable my neck and shoulders are.* In fact, after considerable practice it was determined *both* of them possessed delightfully sensitive and sensual necks and shoulders.

Rhonda eventually allowed Gwen to kiss, lick, and suckle her breasts even though she didn't permit Marc to taste her. *I absolutely* love *having my breasts kissed, and I can tell Gwen* loves *doing it! It makes me groan and absolutely melt inside, causing my hips to involuntarily twitch and making me wet. I do it as much for my own benefit, as my dear girlfriend's benefit.*

Gwen was absolutely infatuated with Rhonda's breasts, so playing with, kissing, tickling, and suckling her lovely mammaries worked for both of them. It was not unusual for them to fall asleep in each other's arms, Gwen still gently suckling Rhonda's breasts and wake up during the night the same way.

Rhonda's best friend was very shy and inhibited about her breasts because her cup size was a B, maybe about the size of a teacup, with a huge, long, puffy nipple easily over an inch long and about the diameter of a thick pencil. Gwen was sure her breasts were malformed and ugly, in comparison with Rhonda's classically beautiful pear-shaped, full breasts that fit very nicely into a 34C bra a month before Gwen reached a B cup.

Not wanting her dear friend to feel inferior, they gave affectionate, playful names to each of Gwen's nipples. The left one was Little Marc, the right Marc Little. Rhonda would spend long intervals playing with and enjoying both Marcs.

Each time, something new was added to their tryst, a little more time kissing the neck and shoulders, exploring caresses of the arms, trailing fingers through each other's hair, giving soft nipple bites, sucking fingers and toes, rubbing and kissing one ass cheek or the other, etc. Nightgowns were slowly removed over the course of many hours of exploration and experimentation.

In addition, Rhonda told Gwen one summer night, "You love my breasts. Good. My breasts love you, too. I love your delicious ass!" she quipped, flipping the ballet dancer over onto her belly with a mock protest and a squeal, kissing both cheeks firmly, and then giving them a sharp smack with her hand.

Smack!

Gwen had taken up ballet four years ago and had a dancer's muscled legs and fine, tight, round ass. Rhonda truly admired her great ass and legs, and was not shy in admitting it.

"You have one fine ass, Miss Gwendolyn O' Rourke!"

Smack!!...followed by a dozen sexy, kissy smacks on the reddened areas...Smack!...another dozen kisses...more squeals...

Pretty panties were left on although intertwining legs together and rubbing between the other's legs with thighs, up and down, while being kissed and explored was the next step in the sensual journey and would result in pleasurably honey-soaked undies, well worn, in the middle of the night.

At first Rhonda and Gwen considered experimenting with each other to be just a friendly and exciting way to learn about ourselves and what pleases and satisfies them, in preparation for guys.

But over time, it had also become a friendly affair, with shared emotions and intimacies that progressed at a mutually comfortable, glacial pace. Girlfriends with benefits, so to speak.

It was after one of those incredibly intensive sexual experiences that Gwen stated, simply, 'You know I love you, right?" to which Rhonda just smiled and replied, "Of course. I love you, too. I thought you knew it a long time ago."

All of the emotions were there with Gwen that were missing with Marc.

Chapter Nineteen

Rhonda felt a sigh of relief as Marc continued to visit her at home. *I'm so much more comfortable here, rather than in the woods.*

If her parents didn't go to the Country Club on a particular evening, Rhonda would claim she was tired or was studying for a test, retiring early to study in her bedroom around eight. Waiting till her parents were watching television or having cocktails in the living room, she would exit carefully and quietly out her bedroom door into the back yard to meet Marc at the gate and later return the same way forty minutes later.

Sneaking around makes me uneasy, but for Marc, it's definitely worth it.

Marc would tell his parents he was studying at the library or playing basketball at the gymnasium. Then he would take an exciting anticipatory ten-minute bike ride to Rhonda's house or a twenty-minute walk/jog. After their tryst, he would easily be back at his home in plenty of time for his ten o clock curfew.

When Marc visited Rhonda's house around eight, Gwen would watch from her front porch next door until she saw Marc enter Rhonda's house. Then she would wait for him to leave about a half hour or so later.

I can only imagine *what they are doing,* she would think to herself.

As soon as Marc would leave, Gwen, telling her mom she was going next door for schoolwork, would rush over to Rhonda's house to get the entire, detailed, often hour-long report of what happened, how it occurred, and how it felt as it was happening.

Chapter Twenty

Rhonda's willingness to have sex-exploration time with him was definitely a positive thing for Marc, to his way of thinking. As none of his buddies, or even any of the juniors or seniors as far as anyone knew, were getting good blow jobs and some fine titty play three more times a week, his reputation as a ladies' man and Big Man on Campus was moderately enhanced.

After hearing so many sensual things about Rhonda, Robby began to look for her in the halls to see if Marc's descriptions of her matched her appearance. They did, and he started to look at her in a different, possibly sexual way.

Marc hasn't said she's his girlfriend, so Rhonda is technically still a free agent. She's a cute JV cheerleader with a nice smile and a curvy little figure. Plus, she's apparently pretty horny, too.

Robby mentioned Marc's incredible good luck to a couple other JV guys they knew in the locker room, and they didn't believe him, either. It was almost unheard of for a sophomore to upstage the other junior and senior athletes with the girls, so they didn't give him much credence for the first couple weeks.

Marc began to strut a little, then a lot. Talking to a couple juniors and even seniors about having oral sex with Rhonda put him on their level as a stud because he was speaking from experience, which gave him credibility. As they came to believe he was telling the truth, Marc was accepted, which was what he really wanted, as hard as it was to believe. *Being accepted as an equal by upperclassmen is a real feather in my cap.*

The possible effects on Rhonda and her reputation rarely ever crossed his mind. He never really intended for more than a handful of trusted guys to know, but somehow the cat had been let out of the bag, and wasn't going to being stuffed back in! *Too late now! A bunch of guys I don't know or trust are talking! A couple of those guys are real jerks, junior and senior arrogant assholes!*

I don't know of anything I can do now to stop the talk. As more guys became aware he decided to just enjoy his newfound status as BMOC. *Maybe this won't be such a big thing and this potential problem will just blow over.*

His confidence soaring, Marc began making casual, overtly sexually suggestive remarks to other girls in loud whispers in the halls, not really caring if they responded positively or not because he knew Rhonda would pleasure him to completion later that day.

I am being cool, nonchalant, confident, and self-assured.

The girls didn't respond favorably for the most part and some, if not all, were offended. Marc demonstrated a lot of attitude, which some girls liked, but it was a Bad Attitude. He was oblivious and unconcerned, even as his reputation as an indiscrete and immodest jerk quickly grew among the girls. He was sure his reputation as a Big Man on Campus, a Romeo, was growing—and it was, but not in a positive way.

Without really knowing it, he had become a jerk.

One highly educational week led to another, then a third, and a fourth.

The third week, one of Rhonda's casual girlfriends asked how she could put up with Marc, but didn't give any specifics.

Surprised to hear her say anything about Marc and her, Rhonda was pleased to hear it. *Maybe he has been telling people I'm his girlfriend!*

The next day, a tall guy she later learned was on the baseball team passed her a folded note in the hallway then walked away without a word.

Is it a love note? An unknown admirer? It only read 34C.

Never having met or spoken to him before, Rhonda didn't know what to make of it. Later she learned from some older girls his name was Curt and he had something of a reputation as an arrogant, self-centered jerk who also happened to be the star pitcher on the varsity baseball team. *I'm flattered and excited to get the attention of a varsity player, a star baseball upperclassman, but don't really know what to do about it.*

After discussing it with Gwen at some length, she decided it would be better to wait and see what the story was with the older guy, Curt. Rhonda was torn but not averse to having two boyfriends at one time. *After all, Marc hasn't told everybody I am his girlfriend, yet, as far as I know, so it isn't official.*

At the same time, she did like Marc and wanted to be his official girlfriend, but he was resisting, so it was decided to keep her options open and see what happened.

On Friday of the fourth week, Rhonda found out from some other girls Marc had been bragging to a half dozen of his buddies about her, telling them how good she was at oral sex, how fine her titties were, how she swallowed without protest—and that her bra size was 34C.

Rhonda was crushed.

The word quickly spread around school, and a couple guys she barely knew started coming up to her making rude comments about her oral skills and asking her for blowjobs in loud whispers that easily reverberated down the crowded halls.

Embarrassed, hurt, and disappointed, Rhonda felt betrayed by Marc.

Confronting Marc, crying, after school in the parking lot, he was surprised but didn't deny it, saying there had never been any intent to hurt her or her reputation, insisting vehemently only good things about her excellent kissing, great boobs, and excellent cock-sucking skills had been discussed.

In his mind, from his perspective, he considered his comments about her as a positive thing for her, like a good reference, a compliment, something a guy would be glad to receive, like her telling her girlfriends he had a big cock, was a great kisser, and a fabulous lover!

How can she complain about me complimenting her??

Chapter Twenty-One

Rhonda was seriously thinking of dropping out of school or transferring to another school to avoid the embarrassment and humiliation, but didn't know how to tell her parents about it without telling them about her sexual episodes with Marc.

The entire weekend after she found out about and confronting him was spent in Gwen's bed, crying inconsolably.

"I loved him! Couldn't he tell? What more could I have done? Why would he do something like that? I did almost everything he asked me to do! I pleased him completely every time! I let him take my top off! He was the first one I let take my top off! The only one! I wanted Marc inside me, too. Why would he tell everybody? I can never show my face at school again! He made me look like a slut! A tramp! Now everybody at school knows everything about me! I never did one thing to hurt him! I hate him! What a fucking jerk!"

Rhonda's chest physically hurt from the sobbing and the poignant pain.

Gwen struggled to console Rhonda. *I don't know what to say or do to make my dear girlfriend feel better.* She hurt for her best friend, as the emotional pain was intense. They fell asleep after several hours of Rhonda's brokenhearted sobbing.

All Gwen could do was to hold her until she cried herself to sleep. Both of their nightgowns were soaked at the top and the shoulder. Awakening a couple times the first night, Gwen heard Rhonda whimpering and wailing, tossing and turning in her fitful sleep.

There was no energy or desire to get out of bed Saturday morning, so Gwen explained to her mom that Rhonda had broken up with her boyfriend, without all the details. Shirley read between the lines, called Teresa, explained the situation, and got permission for the girls to spend another night together.

The intensely felt emotional discussions, sadness, and tearfulness continued all day and deep into the night. Gwen's mom made lunch and dinner for them and brought it to their room. She saw the pain in Rhonda's eyes and offered her condolences.

I have never seen her so distraught before.

Gwen tried to be a good listener and agreed multiple times in a wide variety of ways that Marc was an inconsiderate jerk who had no concern about the feelings of others.

Rhonda cried herself into a fitful, tearful, whimpering, and wailing sleep three times that day in Gwen's arms. Listening and holding her was all her dear girlfriend could do. There are few shortcuts in the mourning process.

Somewhere deep into the dark Sunday morning, Gwen awoke to find Rhonda lying on her chest, awake, breathing quietly but not crying.

"Are you awake, baby? Are you okay?"

"Yes," Rhonda replied, "I'm better now"

"Do you want to talk some more?" Gwen asked.

"Yes. I want to tell you something I've decided"

"What is it, baby? What have you decided?" fearing the worst. *Hurt Marc? Kill Marc? Suicide? Quit school? Run away?*

Pushing her face up to Gwen's, an inch away, Rhonda looked deeply into her eyes and revealed her firm, final decision with passion, intensity, sadness, and some anger: " Marc betrayed me. I will *never* allow *any* guy to hurt me like that again...*Ever*!"

The fire in her eyes was visible to Gwen even through the blackness. There was unmistakable determination and resolve in her voice. The decision had been made, and it was irreversible.

Face to face with Gwen in the darkness, Rhonda went on. "Marc was cute, and I enjoyed him a lot. We learned a lot about each other. I loved him, but he never loved me back. He was using me to make himself feel better. I cared about him a lot more than he cared about me, and knowing that really *hurts*."

I'm relieved to not hear any of my worst-case scenarios are going thru Rhonda's head, Gwen thought with relief. Having no idea what to say or do, she just kept quiet and listened.

A two-minute silence followed while Rhonda gathered her thoughts.

"So you see why we have to rename your boobs. Marc Little and Little Marc no longer exist, since Marc no longer exists," she explained with a wan little smile. She was making a weak attempt at humor in the process of slamming the emotional door on Marc.

"I was thinking, since your middle name is Rose, maybe we should rename them as Rose Little and Little Rose! What do you think?" she asked as the beginnings of a little grin started to show itself.

It is good to see my dear friend smile again, after all the sadness and pain, so Gwen replied with a smirk, "Okay, then, Rose Little and Little Rose it is! Damn straight!"

"Now I know the only one who really loves me, besides my family, is you, Gwen. You have always been there for me when I needed you, and I love you for that!" Rhonda said, leaning over to emphasize the point with a kiss full on her girlfriend's mouth.

Rhonda had told Gwen she loved her many times in the past on various occasions, but this time there was something different about it, a seriousness and intensity she was glad to hear because a romantic girl crush on Rhonda had been developing inside over the past several months.

The 'Thank-you-for-being-there-for-me' kiss soon gained passion, tongue, and intensity as Rhonda started cupping Gwen's face in her hands and depositing light affectionate kisses all over. Strategic warm kisses rained softly down her neighbor's neck and shoulders, inciting serious groans of pleasure to escape her throat.

*I **know** how Gwen likes to be kissed.*

Both Roses began to enjoy a manual massage which turned into a knowing, gentle, yet firm, warm, and sensual mouth massage after five minutes.

Awash in romantic and sexual delight, lightning bolts of pleasure coursed up and down Gwen's body as Rhonda stroked and caressed her from head to toe while softly suckling Little Rose. Straddling the redhead's right leg, rubbing her thigh up and down the crevice between her girlfriend's extremities, the dancer's hips began to twitch uncontrollably while Little Rose was delightfully tongue-tantalized. Rhonda soon felt overflowing moisture on her own thigh.

112

Realizing Gwen's honey pot was soaking her pretty, black, lacy panties, Rhonda slowly slid her right hand down her best friend's very kiss-sensitive belly to the waist band of her enticing bikini undies and continued moving lower.

One second later and four inches lower, Gwen grabbed Rhonda's right wrist with her left hand and held it for a few seconds, looking her best friend deep in the eyes; releasing her wrist with a deep groan the redhead eased back onto the bed, delirious.

Both knew one of the final boundaries in their deepening relationship was about to be expanded and crossed, putting them in new, uncharted territory.

Continuing to sweetly tongue Gwen's big nipple back and forth, Rhonda's hand reached the overflowing lubrication dripping from the soaked panties. Putting all four fingers into the valley, Rhonda stroked up and down twice before pulling her fingers back out, drenched. Each digit was licked and sucked in turn, until no more sweetness remained.

"Baby, you are delicious! And soaking wet!" Rhonda whispered, savoring her essence. "I love it! I want more!" Dipping her fingers once again into the honey-soaked panties, the process was repeated.

Speechless with passion, Gwen was unable to do any more than just groan repeatedly, twist her head from side to side, and let her hips do a sexy samba to a rhythm she had never really felt before. *Its embarrassing to admit, even to myself, that I'm so wantonly willing to be pleasured with no desire to protest.* Her surrender to the ultimate, mounting pleasure and eventual thundering, electrified, shuddering satisfaction was imminent, and complete. A permanent smile was plastered on her face, a continuous moan resonated in her throat, and her eyes were clamped shut, failing to focus whenever an occasional futile opening effort was made. *Oh no!...Oh Yes! YES!...ummhmm...*

"Oh, baby…God yes! Yes!!..."

Sliding her hand down Gwen's abdomen the third time, Rhonda' slipped her fingers inside the waistband and right into a thick red bushiness. Glancing up to see if it was okay for her hand to be in the redhead's panties, it became apparent her absolute best girlfriend was beyond protest or resistance, eyes closed, head jerking from side to side, hips moving up and down, lost in waves of incredible current and anticipated pleasures.

Taking Rose Little gently in her mouth, Rhonda proceeded to add a direct, gentle clitoral massage to the cascading symphony of other lightning-bolt pleasures Gwen was experiencing. Lightly rubbing her clit in small circles about the size of a quarter, Rhonda massaged her best friend just like she was pleasing herself, a feel and rhythm well known to her. *It works incredibly well for me at home, so I'm pretty sure it will be freakin' out-of-this-world fabulous for Gwen, too!*

Seven or eight gentle but firm circles with the tips of her middle and index fingers were followed by a dip into the honey slit, top to bottom, one knuckle deep, three or four trips, top to bottom, then back to the circular massages at the top.

Rhonda kept track of her process: *Slit to the clit, repeat as necessary until orgasm.*

Gwen's thunderous finale arrived soon after, pleasing both of them immensely, too. *Oh My God!!!...oh!!! Oh!...OH!!...*

"Jesus, that was fucking great!" Gwen exhaled, a minute later, when her breath and senses returned.

"That was fabulous, baby! I love watching, hearing, feeling, and making you come! Let's do it again! I know you can do it!"

Immediately, the gentle, digital, circular massage was again applied until Gwen's second shuddering Big O arrived a few moments later. Rhonda was also more than pleasantly surprised and pleased because Gwen had never had back-to-back orgasms in the past. *Once is usually enough! Now it's just a good start!*

Being a firm believer good things come in threes, Gwen's drenched panties were pulled down past her ankles and left in a soggy heap at the bottom of the bed, Spreading the redhead's legs, Rhonda slid in between, and implemented sensual strokes, kisses, and caresses up and down her inner and outer silky thighs for five minutes, until finally peeling back the petals of her blossoming womanhood to conduct a very effective sixty-second loving lingual massage. *My whole body is exploding with pleasure!! From deep inside me! Everywhere! I can't stop! Oh no-o-o-o...*

"I love tasting you and pleasing you!" Rhonda gleefully admitted afterward. "You are the bestest and tastiest girlfriend there could ever be!"

That night, a kiss on the lips took on a whole different meaning for both of them, especially when it became a French kiss.

Gwen was forced to put her pillow over her face so her little sister sleeping across the hall would not hear her shrieks, squeals, screams, and orgasmic groans of pleasure and satisfaction. *I want to thank Rhonda effusively as soon as my orgasmic quivering is finished, but I'm just too freakin exhausted and overwhelmed to speak!*

Once the trembling stopped and Gwen could manage to summon the atoms of energy necessary to utter coherent words, she exclaimed, "That was fucking marvelous! I love you! I couldn't stop coming. I almost ate the fucking pillow!"

Smiling with her own satisfaction, Rhonda climbed up Gwen's belly and across her chest so they were again face to face.

"I couldn't stop tasting you either! You are delicious, baby! I am so glad you enjoyed it, too. You are my best, tasty love!

"Fuck Marc! Who needs him? He's a fucking jerk! We don't! He's history."

So they slept the peaceful and satisfied sleep that lovers do, in each other's arms. The next, long-awaited, inevitable liberating boundary had been successfully traversed, and re-set anew.

At dawn Gwen awoke, re-energized, rolled a soundly sleeping Rhonda onto her back, tongue-teased and tasted her breasts, kissed her way slowly down her belly, pulled her panties down to her ankles, then off, slid across her thighs into the center, gently spread her legs, and affectionately, passionately, gladly, greedily, and gratefully consumed her.

Rhonda awoke from her deep and satisfying sleep with a highly pleasurable, trembling orgasmic explosion from who-knows-where even before she was really awake! *Literally, it came out of nowhere! What a delightful and delicious way to start the morning!*

Once more-fully awake, Rhonda became gradually aware she was still in Gwen's bed. Her eyes opening slightly she glanced down at her spread legs, seeing a freckled smiling face peeking at her from above a familiar bush.

"Good morning, baby!" A big smile was on the redhead's beaming face.

Closing her eyes, Gwen's face disappeared into the bush again, and Rhonda felt a fabulous, soft, warm French kiss slowly starting to work its magic again.

Laying back in the bed Rhonda closed her eyes too, and with a smile and a groan, molten lava coursing thru her veins, she no longer withheld her pleasure and satisfaction, and surrendered completely to the tingling, tantalizing, and tickling tasting of her first real lover.

Oh My God! I'm coming again!! I can't fucking believe it!

Quickly grabbing the pillow and holding it to her face so she wouldn't awaken the entire house, a lingual electrode dipped into Rhonda's magical female love receptacle repeatedly until her inner essence could absorb no more. Overloading her pleasure pathways, the explosion temporarily short-circuited her connection to reality, elevating her to a sublime and universally-welcomed, heavenly pleasure plane.

"Ah…..ieeee!" she squealed into the pillow. *I can't stop myself from screaming!* She was trying to say "I'm coming," but the constant barrage of pleasure would not allow more than one syllable at a time.

Groans and moans of pleasure became well-muffled shrieks and screams within the throes of a loving ecstasy neither female had ever known, which eventually subsided into a special quiet bonding moment.

"I love you, baby," Rhonda stated, simply, after her voice and senses returned and she stopped quivering.

Hearing Rhonda loved her, loved tasting her, and just being with her, Gwen sincerely returned the compliment. *It has an even stronger and truer ring to it.*

Gwen was mildly surprised to find she liked the taste of Rhonda, too, and proud she could lingually bring her to orgasm. *I've never brought anybody other than myself to orgasm, and I am extremely pleased and proud of myself now it has happened!*

Rhonda being Gwen's first tasting was just icing on the cake, so to speak, as they were already special girlfriends. This latest adventure just made their friendship that much more special. Of course, Rhonda was readily and easily orgasmic, so it really didn't take a lot of lingual skill to get her off. They were intimate girlfriends, with real feelings and affection for each other, so she was perfect for Gwen.

Rhonda knew that she and Gwen honestly and sincerely communicated as lovers and friends in a way that had been missing with Marc. With Gwen, she was finally experiencing what she had been craving: the romantic part of an intimate relationship.

Chapter Twenty-Two

The acute emotional pain of Marc pretty much disappeared overnight, but the residual sadness and feelings of loss lasted a while longer. Thanks to Gwen, the residual aching related to the breakup and loss was lessened and made almost tolerable.

I've regretfully lost one love and gladly gained another in a weekend.

With Gwen, Rhonda didn't have to restrain her sexual responses out of fear she might like it too much and become pregnant or contract a sexually transmitted disease. *Being with Gwen truly sets me sexually free, liberates me. We are exploring new boundaries, new opportunities… truly liberated ladies.*

In addition, Rhonda didn't have to worry about Gwen thinking she was a slut or a tramp because it was clear they were both incredibly hormonal and horny, with active fantasy lives. *There are fewer secrets between us, as the level of trust and intimacy is already high.*

Perhaps best of all, the level of emotional intimacy and sharing between them deepened. There was time taken before, during, and after their almost-daily regular sex for sharing and snuggling. Pillow talk finally became as integral a part of a relationship as Rhonda always heard it should be.

Sometimes it's lovemaking; other times it is just great sex! For each to have ten strong orgasms in a night was not unusual, especially at the start of their love affair. Over time, they both realized, as great as that many orgasms were, it was exhausting, too, and left little energy for quality snuggling afterward.

As their relationship evolved, they found three or four shuddering orgasms per night, for each, worked better, especially if they had been preceded by at least an hour or more of teasing foreplay. *Experimenting with carrots and cucumbers is great fun!* Waking up to a terrific, trembling "O" in the black of the night was truly delightful, immensely satisfying, and not really unusual.

Instead of searching for a rubber, like I did with Marc, I will begin subtly checking around, with Gwen, to find where we can get a dildo and a vibrator. I made some money babysitting for the Harris kids across the street and want to invest it in a play toy. A whole new set of questions and possibilities arose.

No-boundary sex was a first for them both. It was not completely unexpected because Gwen and Rhonda had been having limited exploratory sensual activities together for months and it was just a matter of time until all of the borders were crossed.

They had both fantasized and talked about what no-boundary sex with another special female would be like, in the past, and agreed only a girl they liked would do, which kind of locked them into having sex with each other, to the disappointment of neither. It became an eventual given, a mutually understood conclusion, where the only question was *when* it would happen. Neither was in any rush. They liked each other and enjoyed gradually pleasing each other, so it wasn't an urgent problem.

In addition, since both young ladies were smart, they also began soundproofing their bedrooms as much as possible to diminish the frequent shrieks and screams of pleasure regularly coming from there. Gwen moved her bed from next to the door to along the opposing wall, the farthest possible spot away from the door. Putting her radio next to the door she tuned in some Easy Listening romantic music at a moderate volume all night, telling her mom it helped her go to sleep.

120

Rhonda did the same things with her bedroom two weeks later.

To further avoid discovery of their affair, they encouraged both little sisters to spend the night together at one house on the weekends while Gwen and Rhonda would stay at the other. There were a couple close calls when the screams of pleasure and orgasm became piercing, occasionally, but fortunately it was usually early in the morning and nobody came to investigate.

Neither Rhonda nor Gwen felt the least bit ashamed or regretful. To them, it was a natural evolution of their relationship to its natural conclusion. The physical and emotional intimacy over the years had come to fruition. New frontiers were being explored.

Rhonda knew deep inside there were dozens of guys and girls she found attractive at school alone, not to mention the lake and the mall. She and Gwen agreed their relationship had become special because they loved and trusted each other, shared common interests, and had a long history as dear friends who covered each other's backs, which made her, and their relationship unique.

Rhonda accepted that she was attracted to both sexes. *Marc is my first guy crush and Gwen is my first gal crush.*

Starting an affair with Gwen didn't resolve the issues at school, however. Rhonda feigned an illness and took a week off school to compose herself emotionally. Her BFF collected her homework assignments, took them home, and turned them in as they were completed.

In addition, for the rest of the school year Gwen would be Rhonda's lookout as she went from class to class, so Marc could be avoided. These little favors were huge because Rhonda was not emotionally ready to see Marc face to face. Again, Gwen came to the rescue.

Chapter Twenty-Three

Fortunately for Rhonda, two of her favorite female teachers heard about Marc's comments and behavior thru the ladies' high school grapevine the Monday after the Friday blowup and decided to intervene on her behalf.

Mrs. Alvarez, her English teacher, and Mrs. Moffett, the Home Economics instructor liked Rhonda, believed she was just a nice, normal, hormonal young girl looking for romance, involved with a slightly older, basically decent, but still young and inexperienced, newly cocky jerk/jock, and decided Marc and several like him needed a lesson in social and sexual decorum.

Gathering the most influential, and popular female leaders, athletes, band members, cheerleaders, and club presidents in school at the end of the school day that Monday the teachers proposed a solution. In Mrs. Alvarez's classroom, the group decided to teach all the guys in their school a valuable lesson the would-be Romeos would not soon forget!

A tacit agreement among all the girls in school was made to give Marc the ice-cold shoulder for the rest of the school year, almost three months. It would only last until school was out for the summer, but he didn't know it at the time. As far as he knew, it could have been forever.

The other girls who were also having sex with their boyfriends felt threatened by guys like Marc and wanted to send a strong message to all the other would-be Casanovas in school. They were going to let them know in no uncertain terms they didn't approve of their overt behavior, so the women unofficially decided among themselves to make a lasting impression on Marc, and vicariously on all the other similar-thinking guys in school, by making him a social pariah.

Word flashed throughout school in an afternoon among the gathered girls, and by the next morning Marc had *no* friends, male or female.

The girls agreed it would be hard to enforce a freeze-out for much longer than the end of the school year, and certainly not during the summer, but they didn't let on to Marc. *Let him stew in his sins for a while.*

God! I can't get a date and virtually no girls will even talk to me, thought Marc. *Most guys won't talk to me either, for fear of getting the cold shoulder, too.* The ones who did talk to him seriously regretted it afterward, as the refrigerator punishment was swift, cold, and harsh.

Party invitations were withdrawn. Buddies to cruise the mall, go to the movies, or hang out with him were impossible to find. Guys on the baseball team spoke to him in the course of a practice or a game about baseball or baseball strategy but not any more than necessary. Girls who talked to him or socialized with him were also given the cold shoulder and publicly ostracized.

The ice pact was amazingly effective. He was unofficially on everybody's Shit List.

Marc's sister told his mom what he had done, of course, so there was little support even within his own family. His dad just shook his head in passing. He didn't want to get involved.

The girls rallied around Rhonda as the party who had been wronged, with the intent to nip that particular insensitive, thoughtless, and socially unacceptable behavior of Marc's in the bud as much as possible.

Knowing that if it could happen to Rhonda, it could just as easily happen to them, they got on board, even those girls who were jealous of Rhonda as a JV cheerleader, popular, generally happy, adventuresome, and smart girl.

"It's super great of the teachers and other girls to do this for me, but I really just want to put it all behind me, forget it, and move on, Gwen. I'm so embarrassed to think everyone in school knows my sexual history with Marc."

The girls took her experience with Marc as a natural, normal phase of life most of them were going through, in one phase or another. Rhonda had just set the tone and was a leader in their sexual evolution. They could, and would, learn from her mistakes.

The school's united feminine frozen front made the message clear: if you blatantly talk about us sexually to your buddies or anybody else, you will be lonely and horny for a long time!

The guys bided their time until the Ice Winter had passed, but didn't forget Rhonda was now sexually active, experienced, horny, and probably eventually available once the storm had passed. They would be *very careful* with her though.

To herself, Rhonda was pleased Marc thought her oral skills were worth bragging about, but it was a small solace compared to the emotional pain Marc inflicted, and she couldn't enjoy that facet for a couple months, until the pain, disappointment, and abject sadness had subsided.

Since she did have some fond memories of him, Rhonda occasionally felt sorry for Marc as he was socially shut out, but her nostalgic sympathetic feelings were quickly squelched when remembering how much embarrassment and humiliation he had caused her by his actions.

In the end, both she and Marc would survive and move on, knowing they had each learned a painful lesson.

During those last three months of the school year, everybody was polite to Rhonda and supportive, but not particularly friendly or fun. None of the boys flirted with her, tried to ogle her, or even tried to bump into her to get a feel of her breasts or butt. *I actually miss the dirty jokes and little comments they used to make!*

Being the girl who had brought an Ice Age down on one of their buddies, they didn't want to take a chance on the iciness and isolation falling on them, too.

The girls, although supportive, were a little less friendly with her, too. They were anxious for the end of school so they could resume their own sexual and romantic activities; the guys, even the boyfriends, of course, had been pretty much afraid to approach or touch them for fear of offending them during the Ice Age.

Careful to be proper and respectable during those weeks, Rhonda focused on schoolwork, not going to any parties or dances, and not even flirting.

Thank God I have Gwen.

Rhonda also learned to try to choose boyfriends who were more discrete and trustworthy, which happened naturally as the guys got older, more experienced, and wiser.

Even in high school, girls usually knew to be discrete and keep each other's secrets. Although they often shared intimate details with close friends, they didn't usually brag about their exploits in public. As Rhonda now knew firsthand, it is the girl's reputation that will suffer from public exposure, not the guy's.

Conversely, most teenage guys hoped their female sexual partners *would* brag to the world about their sexual skills! *It never hurts to have a lot of good references! Spreading it around that I am a great kisser, have a* huge *schlong, and really know how to use it to pleasure girls will probably open up many more sexual opportunities for me!*

Chapter Twenty-Four

While Rhonda was thankful and fortunate to have Gwen as her best friend and confidant during those painfully difficult months after Marc, her dear friend was also glad and grateful for their special relationship.

It was Rhonda who defended Gwen when the Rich Bitches, the mean girls, began bullying and deriding her in the hall in ninth grade after the very bright redhead had gotten excited when she saw on the bulletin board her grades - all A's again, the Dean's List, with all accelerated classes!

"I did it! I didn't know if I could do it, but I did! In the whole school there are only three of us who got all A's taking Honor courses!" she excitedly exclaimed to anybody and everybody who would listen in the packed and noisy hallway.

The Rich Bitches gathered around then, and made loud, nasty remarks about Gwen. "Isn't *she* special? She thinks she's better than us just because she cheated and got better grades! Nobody will ask her out because she has no real figure and a flat chest, so she had plenty of time to study. *Some* of us actually *have* social lives and can't spend all our time *studying*. She has probably never had a date in her life, and never will!"

It was a gang mentality of bullies and bitches.

Cruising down the crowded hall to meet Gwen between classes, Rhonda heard those remarks and saw the Rich Bitches, and her best girlfriend. Quickly sizing up the situation, she veered over to take her excited neighbor by the arm and steer her down the hall, while loudly remarking, "Come with me, Gwen. These Rich Bitches are just jealous because they will *never* make the Dean's List themselves."

Before the Rich Bitches could respond, Rhonda added, "And she got her grades from hard study, without paying anybody off or blowing anybody!"

This stopped the Rich Bitches in their tracks because they didn't think anybody knew Denise, one of the main Rich Bitches, had blown Ruben Hirsch, one of the smartest guys in school, and paid him twenty bucks so he would write a term paper for her in History class. Only a precious few Rich Bitches were supposed to know that juicy story.

Even fewer people were supposed to know Ashley, the leader of The Rich Bitches had seduced and blackmailed the Civics teacher. It was supposed to be Top Secret, too. The Rich Bitches had a serious security leak requiring immediate attention, even before exacting revenge on Rhonda.

Chapter Twenty-Five

Ruben Hirsch was readily acknowledged by most of his classmates as one of the five smartest students in school. It was also well known in school, because of his thick glasses, frail, slim physique, shyness, and poor athletic and social skills, he had not had much success playing sports, making friends, or dating girls. He was also an easy and frequent target for bullies. Although his nose was usually buried in a library book about space and the planets, space travel, or NASA, his hormones were alive and well.

He was pleasantly surprised when one of the bleach-blond, tight-sweater Rich Bitches, Denise, was nice to him two weeks before the semester ended, stopping him in the hall after History class.

"Hey Rubin! How are you doing?" a little smile on her face.

"Whaat?" *Denise has never even talked to me before!*

"I need a little favor, Ruben. You are a smart guy and good at history, right? I have been so busy I just haven't gotten around to our term paper that's due in two weeks and could use somebody like you to help me out with it! I'll give you twenty bucks!"

Denise's father was a successful lawyer, and she always had money, drove a two-year-old red Mustang, and had the latest clothes and hairstyles, so the money was no problem for her.

I know it isn't right to ghostwrite her paper, but I think— hope, really—maybe she will say nice things about me to the other girls if I do it. So, with some reluctance he agreed and started working on the ten-page-minimum paper in the city library. The fact Denise was not a nice person was well known to him, but she was being outwardly pleasant to him for now, and he was honestly hoping she might open some social and sexual doors for him. The twenty bucks would also come in handy.

Denise would ask him very sweetly every day about his progress with the project, and he would give her an update.

"Well, how is the paper going, Ruben?" she would ask with a little smile.

I know she's faking her smile, but I still like it.

"I have my own homework to do, first, of course, but it's coming along okay…"

A week before the deadline, when Ruben had completed six pages, about half the project, he learned Denise had made a similar arrangement last semester with Aaron, a very bright bookworm buddy of Ruben's. Afterward, however, Denise had refused to pay Aaron what she had promised, claiming he had gotten several rides in her car, twice to pep rallies and twice home from school, so they were even.

"Car rides," Aaron confirmed, "had never been discussed beforehand in lieu of payment, but I just let it go because I was concerned she would just start rumors and lies about me being gay, having a tiny dick, bad breath, etc., with her girlfriends, who would spread it all over the school."

130

Christ! Denise could pull the same stunt on me, too! So Ruben told her he was stopping work altogether if she didn't pay up front. *She is insulting my intelligence, my one strong suite and only source of pride. I damn sure don't want her playing me for a sucker.* Ruben was pissed at how this dumb slut had not only manipulated Aaron but also because she thought Ruben could be outsmarted by doing the same thing to him.

Bullies and liars were the two things Ruben hated most and he had experienced plenty of both over the years as the butt of their jokes, mean-spirited comments, physical intimidation, and false rumors. Even though it hurt whenever those things happened, he also felt helpless to respond. *I just take it, but I don't forget.* The anger just kept building up.

Denise was becoming desperate with only one week left, yet insisted she wouldn't have the money for another week.

"My monthly allowance arrives next week, on Saturday."

The paper was due on the Friday before.

Is the timing a coincidence? I don't think so.

She seriously underestimated Ruben's intelligence again, as well as his accumulated anger.

This is finally a situation where I am in power, and I am smart enough to know it. The shoe is now on the other foot! Let's see how that bitch likes it!

Ruben didn't believe her allowance excuse and correctly thought she was just trying to manipulate him like she had Aaron. He believed there was considerable leverage on his side, and since it didn't look like any payments were coming his way anyway, Ruben decided to give her another option.

I heard a rumor that Denise is also a slut.

131

And Ruben was plenty horny, so he put two and two together.

"Well, if you can't pay, you'll have to make it up to me another way."

"I'm not gonna screw you, if that's what you mean..."

"No, you can just make it happen for me from a position I'm sure you're very familiar with: on your *knees*," he replied scathingly. "Make up your mind NOW, bitch!!!"

Denise was taken aback, surprised by his angry response. *What the fuck? I have never seen him hostile before. This scrawny little fucking geek is yelling at me! Who the fuck does he think he is? Nobody talks to me that way!*

Although he was not physically threatening or intimidating, the intensity of his rage was considerable.

Screw her! All that work, wasted! That bitch!

He didn't care, and really thought those six pages of research and work were probably done for nothing.

How can I like, understand, and enjoy girls when lying, deceitful, and manipulative bitches like Denise come along?

Denise acted at first like she was offended while, inside, considering her options: *Should I spread some humiliating rumors around school about this nerd?* That had worked with other guys, but realized Ruben might very well have found out about how she had used Aaron last semester. *All Ruben has to do is tell a few teachers about how I had cheated, and my hopes of getting a scholarship to college are shot. Or even worse, I could be suspended or expelled. My parents will kill me!*

132

Next, Denise seriously considered beating him up and taking the paper from him, even if it was only half done, or getting another nerd to do it on an emergency basis!

As Ruben watched Denise squirm, it became clear he had her over a proverbial barrel with only a week until the paper was due. The image came to life in his mind– *bend her over a barrel and bang her slutty brains out, preferably onstage during a pep rally! Sorry slut!*

Denise had unknowingly tapped into years of pent-up anger and hostility in Ruben. Manipulators like her had a way of generally bringing out the worst in people.

She knew there were no intentions of paying him, anyway. *He's just a nerd I can use to make my life easier. What is he going to do when I don't pay him? Hit me with his glasses case? I'll bet he's only about one hundred thirty pounds soaking wet, maybe, without a muscle in sight. I can probably beat him up, if all other options fail.*

But then desperation sank in, and Denise finally realized she was surely going to fail the course. It was too late to start on the paper now, and her basic laziness and total lack of interest in history made the situation worse.

My parents promised me a hundred-dollar reward if I make the Honor Roll, and I'll never make it if I fail history. I don't even want to think about the other, seriously worse, possible consequences.

He had something **she** really wanted, and **she** had something **he** really wanted. She also had the twenty bucks. Her offer was increased to twenty-five bucks, but Ruben just laughed in her face.

"Are you fucking kidding me? Forget it!"

Thirty bucks, as her final offer, drew only a sneer and a nasty laugh.

"No fucking way! Make up your mind, bitch! Now!"

Coming up with no feasible solution, and fearing Ruben might actually turn her in for cheating, Denise decided to agree to his sexual demands, but warned him not to tell anyone about it.

"You're in on this, too," she reminded him, "and can get in just as much trouble as me."

That night, Denise found Ruben way back in the stacks at the city library on the second floor where he usually was camped out. Wordlessly, she began what appeared to be a quick payment on her paper, from her knees.

Ruben was truly surprised she showed up, but glad and excited, too. *She really **is** a slut! Great!* He sensed the upper hand was his for once and was still mad at her because it was clear her intentions were not honorable.

Denise is a user of people. Finally I am getting some revenge on at least one of the users and manipulators in my life! This bitch will be used, and we'll see how she likes it!

Never really expecting her to go through with this, even after agreeing to his terms, Ruben was stunned to see her. Being his first sexual experience, he wasn't sure what to do. *I'm pretty sure I'm going to enjoy it, and I want to make sure Denise knows it, too! She'll know by the end because I have every intention of letting her know, in spades! My gun **is** fully loaded, but I plan to enjoy it for as long as possible.*

Pushing his chair out from under the table, Ruben stood and turned to the left to face her when she arrived. Denise took a quick look around to be sure nobody else was nearby, then knelt, impatiently unzipped his pants, and bent down to engulf him.

Damn! This feels fucking great! Like fireworks are going off in my head! My rocket is preparing to ignite! Going to explode!

Denise gave Ruben good head because, first, she didn't want to be there at all and wanted it over as quickly as possible, and second, she didn't want to be on her knees in front of *him* any longer than absolutely necessary because he was absolutely gloating. *He is in his glory, thoroughly enjoying himself, big time, at my expense! I am being used for his pleasure and satisfaction, and I fucking* hate *it!*

After a minute, Denise became concerned someone might hear Ruben's serious groans and moans, so she paused, took him out of her mouth, and hissed at him under her breath, "Not so loud! Somebody will hear!"

Ruben was finally in charge and knew it. "Shut up and suck, bitch!" he growled low, imitating dialogue he had once read in a contraband book he'd found in the boys' locker room, putting his still-swollen cock back into her mouth. "No swallow, no deal!"

In any other circumstance, Denise might have enjoyed it because he was nicely hung for a guy his size and her hand barely wrapped around it. *This is taking so long! It has to be almost three minutes already. He is enjoying this way too much, and I'm really getting pissed. That puny little punk!*

When Ruben finally let loose, Denise swallowed hard three times but did not milk him dry like she usually did with other guys. *Sexual servicing and minimal relief, getting him off, not draining him to complete satisfaction—that's the goal*, she thought. *He probably doesn't know the difference! Ruben is fucking lucky to be getting relief, that scrawny little fucking geek!*

But Ruben's mind was screaming, *Damn! That feels freaking great!!!! Yes-s-s-s! Hell yes!* ...sinking slowly back into his chair.

After recovering some, Ruben quickly realized he still had her backed into a corner. Turning over the work he'd completed so far, Denise was told he would do one page more at a time, until it was done, only if she would come back every night and make partial payments, one swallow at a time, for each remaining page.

"What? That wasn't the deal! You didn't say anything about repeat blowjobs before! You are changing the rules now! It's not fair, and you know it!"

"Since when are you concerned about doing what is fair, Denise? Ever?...No, I didn't think so."

Ruben is so smug and angry, that little fucking prick!

"Well, what if I don't agree? I will tell all the kids in school you lied to me and changed the deal!"

"Well, I have to admit, first off, it was a nice blowjob... But you are going to tell everybody at school you blew me for a paper? You already have a reputation as a slut, and that will confirm it! And what if the Dean hears about it? It might happen, you know."

He made a couple good points.

After first refusing to agree to his terms, and reluctantly realizing and admitting ratting on him would be a bad decision, she seriously considered beating him up right there, but it *was* the library. Denise *really* wanted the hundred-buck reward, and his silence, so it was worth a few minutes of her time to get a hundred bucks. It just made good business sense.

I will definitely *get this scrawny little fuck back later, when any opportunity arises!*

There was no doubt she hated being used, but after reviewing and exhausting all of her possible options, Denise reluctantly relented. She returned and relieved him every night, as long as he agreed to keep it secret, especially from school officials, even after the paper was turned in and the semester was over.

Ruben agreed to keep their secret, but like Denise, he never intended to keep his word. He told Aaron, "If she can lie whenever she wants, so can I!"

The last night, Denise was surprised to find Ruben there with Aaron. Right then, she knew for sure Aaron had told Ruben about the previous semester. *Oh shit! This isn't good!*

Although Denise still didn't feel bad about having screwed Aaron over, she knew he was probably there for a reason, and his presence meant some payback for him would be demanded. She wanted and needed that last page bad, as it was due the next day.

It was in Ruben's backpack, but she didn't know it.

"You fucked me over last semester, Denise, and you know it! Now it's time for you to make it up to me, bitch!" Aaron sneered.

Denise had a sinking feeling in her stomach. *Crap. Fuck me!*

"I don't like to be talked to like that!" she retorted, acting offended so the upper hand could be regained.

"We don't really care what you like, bitch! We don't like being lied to either! We stick to our agreements, too, and don't try to weasel out of them later like a slutty, lying bitch does! I demand an apology, and I want it right now! Say you're sorry, bitch!"

"I don't apologize to anybody! Ever! And I certainly don't apologize to a couple scrawny geeks!" Denise was trying to bluff her way thru, at this point.

"No apology, no paper. You can apologize, or get on your knees. Make your choice! Now!!" Aaron was incensed.

Best-case scenario for her, she apologizes, and all is forgiven. It will never happen, of course.

I hope she won't apologize and will give both Ruben and me blowjobs, instead. Even if she does apologize, we will change the rules, just like she did, and say, after the apology, blowjobs are still necessary to get the last page! See how Denise likes THAT!

It was made clear she couldn't have the last page until both were serviced. *I don't think I can get the paper away from the two of them, so I guess an extra three reluctant minutes is a small price to pay to get the last page. I just want this to be over!*

Ejaculating in her face, Aaron called her a nasty bitch, which she was. Ruben immediately wished he had done the same, but it was too late.

Not having a handkerchief or a tissue to wipe it off was a problem for Denise because it was her plan to swallow it all, like she did the other times. Licking her lips, she wiped off as much semen as possible with her forefinger and left the library in a hurry, with the seminal mask still visible if anyone looked closely.

The mental picture they memorized of Denise sucking and servicing each of them from her knees, smoothly swallowing Ruben and taking a facial from Aaron, after she had lied to him and screwed him over, was fabulous!!

138

"Goodbye, Denise! There's something dripping from your chin! And in your hair!" Aaron called out to her as she left.

Payback is a bitch! A bitch named Denise!

The guys thoroughly enjoyed watching Denise walking quickly away with a splash of semen in her hair and a serious blob still dripping from her chin. *Priceless!*

Back in school, Ruben and Aaron, being the nerdy but hormonal entities they were, were willing to overlook some of Denise's nastiness and bullying since she did have two saving graces, in their minds: one, she gave good head; and two, she swallowed. Those skills trumped everything else, but they still weren't going to make it easy for her.

They taunted Denise the entire next week whenever they saw her by telling her they would be glad to do future papers for her under the very same conditions —one blowjob per page, each, starting from page one, plus twenty bucks.

"Aaron and I can't decide whether we should get a blowjob each for every page of the paper, or a blowjob for every day it takes to do your paper. What do you think, Denise?" Ruben taunted, waiting for her next to her car in the school parking lot. "Some papers could take as much as a month to finish…"

Pulling her aside in the hall while changing classes, Aaron said in a normal speaking voice, easily audible over the din of students shuffling by, "Ruben has decided next time he wants to ejaculate in your face too, like I did, so you will need Kleenex next time you blow us…"

After a week of daily derision, Denise pulled Ruben aside and hissed at him, "If you get me suspended from school, I'll make sure they all know everything you and Aaron had to do with it. Then, you'll both be suspended, too!"

After that, the boys backed off, but only slightly. They still told all the guys and girls in the Honor Society, including Gwen, the entire story to make sure none of the Rich-and-Nasty bitches would pull a similar stunt again. It was only a small revenge for all the nerds and unpopular kids those girls had made miserable over the years. The geeks also had two reluctant spokesmen and the aura of invincibility with the Rich Bitches had been punctured.

Chapter Twenty-Six

After Rhonda's breakup with Marc, Gwen's obsession with her intensified. Her next-door neighbor became the center of Gwen's universe. Everything was, "Rhonda wore this…Rhonda did that…" excluding of almost everything and everybody else.

Gwen's mom, Shirley, noticed the change in her, and although she understood the situation with Rhonda and the need for a close friend, her belief was once the girls entered high school they should start focusing on guys as future partners and life mates. So, she started limiting Gwen's extracurricular time with Rhonda to four hours during the week and four hours on the weekend.

Being as bright as Gwen was, she quickly realized her mom wanted to hear more stories about guys, rather than Rhonda. As a result, her eldest daughter decided to begin flirting with Ruben, who was in the accelerated classes with her. She was a bit awkward at it, as it was, after all, her very first seduction. However, he was very socially and sexually awkward, and inexperienced, other than his one-sided spiteful revenge experiences with Denise, so he could easily be manipulated however she wanted.

Ruben was thrilled to receive the attention from Gwen although he had no inkling what had changed between them, why it had changed, or where it was headed.

She would never admit it, but Gwen had been impressed with Ruben's results with Denise because he was the only one in the entire school who had confronted the Rich Bitches and won, or at least caused a draw. She didn't like them either.

He was also Gwen's equal in mathematics, elementary physics, and chemistry, although she was more adept at biology and sociology. Ruben was more interested in space and technology. But in general, Gwen enjoyed the intellectual give and take with him, the challenge and stimulation. *Few people can keep up with him, but I can.*

Besides, he would serve a purpose.

Chapter Twenty-Seven

Overhearing Ruben was a big science-fiction fan and especially liked Star Trek, Gwen studied up some and started asking him trivia questions about the television show story lines. She also began reading some science-fiction novels such as Isaac Asimov's *Foundation* and Ray Bradbury's *R is for Rocket* collection of science fiction short stories.

A bunch of the Honor students often went as a group to see sci-fi movies when they were shown at the Essex Theater. When *2001: A Space Odyssey* came to town, Gwen went with them for the first time. There were four guys and two girls in the Honor Society student group that day, including Ruben and Gwen.

The second time Gwen went along, Aaron and Ruben were the only two guys in the group that night. The guys were very comfortable analyzing the action and searching for obscure details about space travel and technology. It became an exciting contest in one-upmanship among the astute male observers without any real input from her.

Gwen had to admit the guys were pretty smart, but was pretty sure she could hold her own. After waiting patiently for her opportunity, she surprised them with a knowledgeable observation about algorithms and computers. As a result, the guys finally included her in the conversation.

Although Gwen thought Aaron was physically more attractive, with his blond hair, blue eyes, and granny glasses, in addition to being incredibly intelligent, he hadn't stood up to Denise until the end. Ruben had set the standard and thus became Gwen's focus.

Subtly flirting with Ruben from time to time, Gwen began trying out various moves, smiles, gestures, and flirtatious comments when Aaron was gone for brief intervals to the restroom or to get a drink at the concession stand.

Ruben was completely befuddled and bewildered by Gwen's flirtations and didn't know what to do in response. No girl had ever flirted with him before, although he had imagined and hoped in his frequent fantasies some girl would.

She keeps smiling at me for no apparent reason I can think of. What does it mean? I know she's smart, probably even every bit as intelligent as me, and in the classroom we are on equal footing, but this smiling, giggling, and flirting behavior is completely alien to me.

Gwen was patient, however. The third Saturday, Ruben's mother took only Ruben and Gwen to the movie and dropped them off, as the other kids couldn't go for one reason or another.

The outing had a lot of dating characteristics because it was just the two of them, together, out in public, sharing the experience by mutual agreement, but it was not an official "date" because neither had really known in advance the others weren't going.

Both were very nervous, Ruben more so, however. His mom gave him ten bucks to buy a large tub of popcorn to share and two Cokes for them both, which he did.

Holding the door open for Gwen as she entered the theater, he was thanked very sweetly. Carrying his Coke in his left hand and the popcorn tub against his body, as they walked down the aisle to their seats, her hand brushed his free right hand, once, then twice. Thinking it was just an accident, but a nice warm, soft accident he liked, Ruben grinned a little and his stomach tightened.

The third time Gwen brushed his hand she grabbed it and slid her hand into his, with a friendly smile.

Ruben was thrilled. *But what does it mean?*

Gwen was tickled. Things were going exactly as planned. *He is certainly my match intellectually, but in the social and romantic arena Ruben is so innocent, defenseless, and inexperienced I almost feel sorry for him.* Yes, he had gotten Denise to give him a few, quick spiteful and vengeful blow jobs, but he had never really experienced all the other really wonderful aspects of romance, sex, relationships, and lovemaking, as far as she knew.

He can be brought along slowly.

A couple times Gwen happened to reach into the popcorn tub at exactly the same moment Ruben did, and with a soft laugh she grabbed his hand and held on to it for a few seconds before releasing it.

After the first time Gwen did it, Ruben did the same with her a couple times. Their hands were greasy with all the butter, which hid the nervous moisture on both of their hands. It was flirty fun for both of them.

I like holding her hand, inside and outside the popcorn tub!

When the popcorn was finished, Gwen thanked Ruben profusely and gave him several napkins to wipe his hands with too.

"The popcorn was delicious! Thank you so much! And the Coke was just perfect to follow it down!" she enthusiastically thanked him with a big smile. Leaning over to give him a quick kiss on the cheek, Gwen ostensibly lost her balance somewhat, and the kiss landed on the edge of his mouth.

Freezing in place, Ruben had no idea what he should do or say.

"Whoops!" she exclaimed, and moved closer to try again, like it had been an accident, while still teetering a little.

Ruben had no idea what she was doing, so he turned his head towards her a little to see—and ran flush into her lips with his.

A shock wave ran right thru him, like he had never known before! *It's like a laser light beam!*

Wow! We are kissing! Once he felt her soft lips on his he pressed forward a little and continued kissing her for the next twenty seconds, until he had to take another breath.

Wow! This is so cool! It's really happening! I'm kissing a girl! Finally! She was smiling, too, and appeared to like it as much as he did, although it wasn't clear to him where he should put his arms and hands.

Seeing his hesitation, Gwen took his face in her hands and kissed him softly on the mouth, her now-clean hands sliding gently into his hair.

Ruben took her lead, cupped her smiling, freckled face in his hands, marveling at how good she felt, and eventually let his fingers slide into her hair.

She's so soft! And warm! I'm kissing a girl! And she's kissing me back! It was a moment and a day they would both remember fondly for the rest of their lives.

The movie was forgotten, as they were both going where neither one of them had ever gone before! *This making-out stuff is pretty cool!*

Gwen's not only smart, but also a good, soft, warm kisser, and she likes me, for some reason, and smells great, too!

They were both sorry to see the movie end and the lights come on.

Ruben held her hand on the way out of the theater and opened the car door for her when his mom arrived. None of this was overlooked by Mrs. Hirsch, who couldn't help a little grin to herself as she acknowledged the fact her son was growing up.

Holding the car door open again for Gwen to exit when they arrived at her house, Ruben was planning to shake her hand goodbye at her front door. Ignoring his proffered hand, Gwen instead quickly reached up and gave him a goodbye peck on the cheek before dashing inside.

Tactfully ignoring the goodbye kiss, Mrs. Hirsch did ask a few general questions on the way home about how the date went. He mumbled something about it going fine before resuming his silent reverie.

Thrilled beyond belief, Ruben needed some time to sort it all out, just like Gwen. *Its all so exciting! What should I do next? Anything? Call her? What would I say?*

Gwen, however, had her mom and Rhonda to talk to and discuss her exciting evening with, in detail, for a thrilling hour.

Ruben had nobody, and he spent the next few hours stewing, tickled and happy, yet confused. *I wish my dad was here.*

Harold Hirsch, Ruben's dad, taught astronomy and physics at the local junior college at night. He was killed when hit driving home by a drunk driver when Ruben was twelve. The shy boy retreated farther into his shell.

Finally, Ruben called Aaron and told him generally what had happened. Neither boy had a clue what it all meant in the overall picture, but they agreed *girls can really be fun, smart, and cool!*

Saturday matinees became a regular outing for Ruben and Gwen, and he started holding her hand at school in the hall. They became something of a couple.

By their sixth date at the movies, Gwen had a Sexy, Soggy Hanky to share afterward with her favorite neighbor.

Excited for her dear friend, there was also a twinge of jealousy there because Rhonda was still being treated way too respectfully at school. Even though her hormones were raging, her only sexual outlet was four one-hour visits per week with Gwen and a Saturday overnighter, and she found herself starting to fantasize about guys at school, rock stars, and teen idols again.

Ruben was the first boy Gwen had ever really liked, held hands with, and kissed, and she would make a point to mention to her mom at least one thing he said or did every day. Over time Gwen grew to like Ruben, his smarts, intelligent sense of humor, gentleness for outcasts like himself, and passion for space and technology a little bit more each day.

But she *loved* Rhonda. Ruben became her "beard," her romantic façade, or obligatory male squeeze, so her mom would allow Gwen to visit Rhonda next door more often. It was win-win for everybody.

As Gwen really began to like Ruben, she kept her mom apprised of the developments as they progressed. Gwen and Shirley were very close and they could discuss just about anything.

After two months of dating Ruben, Gwen told her mom she might be falling in love with him and hinted birth control might be something to consider in the near future.

This, of course, worried Shirley, and she began allowing Gwen to spend more time with Rhonda and less time with Ruben, just as her eldest daughter thought she might.

Soon, however, Gwen told Rhonda she might be falling in love with Ruben, and meant it. He had definitely taken on official "boyfriend" status.

Her fondness for Ruben grew more and more as time went on. She liked him holding her hand in school and in public. *It pleases me to hear Ruben has told his few friends I am his girlfriend.*

Ruben got a job tutoring kids after school to earn money to take Gwen out, and she liked that thought. Gwen continued to find he had a keen wit, sharp intelligence, and a sometimes-biting sense of humor, like her. They both excelled in science and math and neither liked mean or dishonest people, so they had that in common, as well. Gwen also found his empathy and kindness for others quite attractive. Volunteering at the Humane Society one day a week, Ruben fed, watered, and walked the homeless animals, in addition to cleaning out their cages.

As enamored and enraptured as Ruben was with the potential of outer space, he quickly learned exploring hills, valleys, and inner space with Gwen was even more exciting and satisfying. Compared to the vast expanses of outer space he had grown to love while growing up, Ruben grew to love her modestly small areas of inner space, where no man had ever gone before, even more.

We both love exploring new worlds.

Gwen also took a rapidly increasing interest in rocketry, preparatory flight techniques, inner workings, propulsion

149

systems, trajectories, liquid fuels, and the intricacies and sensual subtleties of delivering a seriously satisfying payload, all of which pleased both of them enormously!

Learning from Gwen, Ruben came to appreciate and enjoy the peaks and valleys of her naturally available landscape and the aesthetic, gustatory, olfactory, and geological exploratory drilling possibilities they would present to him from time to time, on a fairly regular basis.

Soon, outer space planetary exploration became their second favorite activity.

Interpersonal space exploration was an activity they could, and would, enjoy together, immensely. Mutual in-flight and post-flight safety was not disregarded in the least. As in any space endeavor and exploration, serious consequences could arise if safety was not a priority.

Gwen accepted and enjoyed Ruben for who he was, and vice versa. She was the first real, close human connection he had made in his peer group not to mention his first romantic affair. *I think her brain and body are both beautiful.*

They went to the Junior and Senior Proms together, as well all the dances and several parties. It was a wonderful first love affair for both of them. *I like Ruben a lot.*

Chapter Twenty-Eight

The summer after Marc, the happening place for teen girls and guys was Lake Lilly, the same local freshwater reservoir where Wesley Bell taught his family to fish. Rhonda, Gwen, her little sister Alice, Rhonda's little sister Patricia, and a couple other teen girls in the neighborhood went at every possible opportunity. It was the high school and junior high school hangout and a place for the girls to show off their new bikinis and blossoming figures.

The guys, of course, would also try to impress the girls with their newly developing muscular bodies, great tans, and nimble athleticism.

Lake Lilly was almost a mile across and had thick green forests around a lot of it. There was a snack bar, a large dock for boats, a boat ramp, a large fenced-in area for weightlifters, and a fifty-car grass parking lot adjacent to the snack bar. Approximately fifty yards of forest had been cleared, up from the water, leaving a white, sandy beach down to the water for over a half mile around the shore in each direction.

On the beach, the girls would flaunt their teeniest bikinis, and the guys would show off and try to get the girls' attention. The modest two-piece bikinis that left home were folded or pinned into tiny four-inch swaths, barely covering the bare essentials by the time the girls got settled on their towels. It was an all-out, female competition to see who was brave enough to wear the least amount of fabric.

From the beginning Rhonda was intrigued by the tanned and muscular weightlifters. Their area was filled with benches, barbells, dumbbells, bars to do chin-ups and pull-ups, and other bodybuilding and workout equipment. There were usually about a dozen mostly shirtless high school athletes in shorts and tennis shoes lifting weights, doing pushups, pull-ups, sit-ups, and various other exercises. Many had big, well-defined muscles. Some had muscles that literally bulged everywhere and great tans all over.

All the muscles, sweat, and bulges mesmerized Rhonda.

I love those big muscles. They are simply beautiful to me. A guy with muscles like that would certainly be strong and powerful enough to protect his girlfriend! Watching the guys flex their muscles sent a definite shudder right through her.

The guys knew it, of course. Flexing their muscles was their way of attracting the females with the promise of power, beauty, and protection, not to mention virile healthy procreation. But none of them consciously thought about that. They just wanted to get laid.

Several groups of junior high and high school girls were usually standing outside the fence and watching, pointing occasionally, giggling, and smiling, but still trying not to stare or be too obvious.

"Oh my God! Look at him! He's *huge!*" Rhonda gushed behind her hand at Gwen. "I wonder if it means his muscles are also *huge* everywhere!" she whispered into Gwen's ear, giggling together at the thought.

Rhonda was awash in a sea of testosterone that matched her own rapidly escalating hormones. She particularly noticed one muscular guy who was obviously very popular, as there were always guys and girls hanging around with him and laughing. He appeared to be pretty well-liked by almost everybody.

Intrigued, she found out from some other girls who hung around there he was Thomas 'Hot Rod' Henderson, and owned a big, loud, fast, and Indian motorcycle with a red gas tank.

Hot Rod had thick, muscular fifteen-inch-around arms and was toned and tanned everywhere, a fact the girls excitedly noted. The girls who were regulars at Lilly Lake also reported he was smart and athletic but had been thrown off the football team for refusing to follow team curfews and other rules. Team sports were not his forte, but he had taken to wrestling, a singular sport, and had wound up second in the state in his weight class in his first full year in the sport.

When Thomas decided to do something, he was determined to do it and do it well. A reputation as a tough, intimidating, macho, sarcastic, undisciplined, and no-nonsense guy who did not suffer fools at all, was well earned. A local bad-ass, in short.

Hmmmm…Rhonda was further intrigued.

Taking the same determined approach to weightlifting as he had with wrestling, after six months of serious workouts before his junior year, Thomas was ripped, and certainly not oblivious to the blossoming teen girls ogling him in a lustful way. On a scale of one to ten, Hot Rod might very well have qualified as a muscular and macho seven point five, or more.

Although he had no particular interest in academics, Thomas maintained a D-minus average so he could stay in school, enjoy the girls, and deal pot. *I'm making seventy-five bucks a week selling weed, sometimes more, and have all the sweet young pussy I can handle. I'm bangin' cheerleaders, Honor Roll students, Rich Bitches, and even good-looking Homecoming Princesses. Life is incredibly good!*

If he flunked out of school, all those opportunities would be lost because Thomas would be banned from school property, so he kept the absolute bare-minimum GPA at all times.

His next-door neighbor he grew up with, Howie, was two years older and belonged to a newly-formed motorcycle gang, The Avengers. *I like their independent, rowdy, and screw-you attitude. Can't wait till I'm old enough to get in with those guys.*

Biding his time, he sold pot bought from Howie at wholesale rates to students at a retail rate, insuring a nice profit margin, until he could become an Avenger.

There were seven hundred and fifty students at Northside High, and Hot Rod was the main pot supplier. He had intimidated a couple other wannabe street guys and a few hippies with his big muscles and bad attitude, running them out of business. That left Hot Rod as the go-to guy for pot and pills.

The red Indian motorcycle was bought with the profits from his first three months in business. Roaring around town on his motorcycle was great fun, burning rubber at stop signs, doing wheelies, and impressing the girls with his muscles, bad attitude, and lack of respect for the law.

When he noticed Rhonda, she was one of a half dozen chicks hanging around the weightlifter's pen. Thomas thought she was pretty cute in her teeny-weeny bikini, and smiled at her.

Flattered when he grinned at her, Rhonda quickly flushed and looked away.

Oh my God! He's looking at me hard, and grinning!

Knowing there were several other cuties present, a lot of them fully blossomed juniors and even some seniors, Rhonda was very pleased he had singled her out.

Since Hot Rod is from the other high school in town, doesn't know and has never even heard about Marc, and has no idea about the Arctic Winter, he isn't afraid to flirt with me.

Thomas might very well have come on to her even if he had known about Marc and the Arctic Winter, she surmised, because he appeared pretty confident and not afraid of anything or anybody, so she shyly smiled back.

Taking her smile as a positive sign he strolled over close to where Rhonda and Gwen were standing, which made both of their stomachs tighten and mouths become dry.

He nodded at Rhonda. "Nice bikini. Do you work out?" which caused her to look down and blush, again.

At that point Gwen turned to her and whispered in her ear that she need to visit the ladies room, NOW!

"I'll be *right back*, Rhonda." She announced, looking quickly at him before hurriedly setting off towards the snack bar.

"No, not really, just cheerleading practice," she murmured.

The permanent, irrevocable, broad, impossible-to-remove smile she had felt before, when meeting Marc, had returned.

"So you're a cheerleader, huh, Rhonda? My name is Thomas, but you can call me Hot Rod! Nice to meet you." flexing his huge left bicep and smiling.

"You must go to Southside High, 'cause I've never seen you at Northside. I always remember the cute ones."

Blushing again, Rhonda looked down, trying to control herself. Looking at him and his muscles, a warm feeling began to spread throughout her body.

Gulp! He thinks I'm cute!

"I'm working on my arms today. Feel my arms and tell me how I'm doing," he instructed, reaching toward her over the waist-high fence and flexing his beautiful, bulging right bicep.

Awash in his glow of testosterone Rhonda didn't really trust herself to touch him, or his bicep, for fear she might like it too much…but did it anyway and found herself trembling with pleasure. Not having touched a guy in almost five months, she quickly realized the muscle and the maleness had been sorely missed! *Jeez, does that feel good! It's huge! Gorgeous!*

Overwhelmed, her eyes suddenly closed and she found herself leaning forward with both of her hands around his big bicep and kissing it gently.

Three seconds later, Rhonda realized what she had done and snapped her eyes open and her head back, looking at him with a somewhat sickly smile of embarrassment and surrender.

Woo-Hoo! This chickadee is ready for plucking!

"Hey—do you like riding motorcycles?"

"Well…um…I never…really…my dad…a couple times…"

Hearing her hesitant reply, he just took her arm, saying, "Your dad has a bike? Great! Come with me! You'll love it!"

She had absolutely loved riding behind her Dad on his motorcycle but had never had an opportunity to ride with a guy her age. *Now I have a chance to ride with Hot Rod! Out of all the girls here, he's chosen me to ride with him!*

Leading her by the hand over to his parked Indian, before she could mount a rational protest, he lifted her up like a feather and set her down astraddle it. Hot Rod showed her where the foot petals were and told her to hold on tight to him, around his waist, when they got going.

It's all happening so fast I can only nod dumbly to acknowledge I understand his instructions.

"This yours?" Hot Rod asked, indicating the T-shirt she'd left on the fence in front of them. "You might want it while you're on the bike. It gets windy." As Rhonda mumbled a barely audible "Thanks," he tossed her the shirt and threw his leg over the red gas tank, gave the kick-peddle a strong kick, and the engine came roaring to life! Reaching around and pulling her arms to encircle his waist, he told her to hang on tight, and they were moving! *I just know am going to absolutely love this!* She said to herself.

Rhonda looked around in the crowd for Gwen to tell her she was going for a ride, but she was still in the ladies room. The only recognizable face was Alice, so she flashed a big smile and waved as they moved into traffic.

That looks like Rhonda riding away on that guy's motorcycle, but I'm not sure! What's she doing riding off with him? Who is that guy? Does she know him? We just got here! Where are my freakin' glasses so I know for sure?

It was all so exhilarating and very groovy, but Rhonda did want Gwen or somebody to know where she was and who she was with for bragging rights as well as safety purposes.

Having seen Alice, and being pretty sure Alice had seen her, too, on the back of Hot Rod's motorcycle, Rhonda felt a little better. She had no idea how long this ride would take, where they were going, or what was going to happen, so it was somewhat scary, but her daredevil side loved it. *Is it just a ride?*

The warm sun on her face felt wonderful and the wind in her hair cooled her off from the summer heat, to some extent. The roar of the engine and the speed of objects hurtling by were both exciting and a little unnerving at the same time.

Driving fast for several minutes down the two-lane highway next to the lake, Hot Rod then turned left off the road onto a hiking path into the woods. Slowing down considerably, he navigated through the shrubs and trees along the well-worn path for a few more minutes until they came to an old, empty, dilapidated, probably abandoned, wooden hunters' cabin. Its windows were broken, trash was strewn in the front yard, and the dented front door was ajar.

Rhonda had no idea where she was, and the excitement of being with Hot Rod and taking her first official bike ride was slowly shifting into fear. When they stopped in front of the cabin, she gently demanded to be taken back to the beach.

"Take me back, okay, Hot Rod?"

Sensing her uneasiness, Thomas replied, "I'll take you back whenever you want. But first, I wanna smoke this joint with you."

Parking the motorcycle, he lifted her off it and led her by the hand into the cabin.

Smoke a joint? With me? Where did that idea come from?

The reassurances he would take her back whenever she wanted calmed her fears somewhat, but Rhonda didn't know whether to believe him or not.

"Do you like to smoke pot?" Thomas inquired with a grin.

"Well...I...never really..." she reluctantly admitted.

He chuckled at her lack of experience. "You'll like it because it's very relaxing. You like being relaxed, right?"

"Well...yeah...I guess so..." Not wanting to look like a complete novice or rookie, she added, "Some of the other kids at school have tried it, and they like it."

"There, see? I know you're gonna like it, too." He smiled and started to roll some pot into a small, thin joint about three inches long.

"This is just a small, skinny one, and we'll be done with it in ten minutes."

Very glad to hear they would soon be leaving, and at the same time, she was very curious what effect the joint would have and what they would eventually do together, if anything.

Why does he want to smoke a joint with me? Is he trying to seduce me?

Hot Rod lit the joint, took a quick drag, and passed it to her, holding it between his thumb and forefinger, keeping the smoke in his lungs for ten seconds or so before slowly releasing it.

I've never smoked a cigarette and think it's a pretty nasty habit, overall, but I'm here and don't want to look so naïve and inexperienced, so I'll just try to copy how he did it. I don't want to embarrass myself completely.

Rhonda took too much in the first puff and wound up coughing and gagging for a full minute, her eyes starting to overflow.

Hot Rod chuckled and took another quick drag. "Take small, quick puffs next time."

She did, and there was no coughing. Laying back on the old dirty mattress on the floor, he took off his shirt, revealing an impossibly broad, muscular chest and ripped abdomen.

Laying back on the mattress, too, a minute later she found herself to be very relaxed and at peace. Another minute later, it felt like she was floating on air. *I'm glad to be here with him. We are relaxing together. He's right. It's* very *relaxing.*

After a couple minutes, Hot Rod rolled over next to her, on his side, then reached out and felt her breast gently thru her T-shirt.

"You have nice titties."

It's a very nice compliment, she thought, and squeezed his huge bicep in return, as he moved closer to kiss her mouth. With his shirt off, Rhonda could see and feel every muscle in his chest, arms, legs, and belly. *He's so impressive, to say the least.*

She had never seen or felt so many muscles, so as he reached under her T-shirt and pulled her bikini top up out of his way and started massaging her bare breasts, Rhonda began feeling his chest, arms, and belly in return.

If he can feel my chest, it's only fair I can feel his chest, too.

Even his lips were strong as he kissed her with growing passion. *He's a good kisser, too! Oh My God!*

"Sit up!" he ordered, and in five seconds her T-shirt was pulled over her head and her bikini top was lying next to her, as she lay back on the mattress. Waves of relaxed pleasure were coursing thru both of them.

He's beautiful. We're meant to be together, Rhonda decided in her smoke-addled state.

Another deep French kiss had her feeling adrift, relaxed, and aroused at the same time. Breaking the kiss to breathe again, he inhaled quickly and slid down to taste her right breast before she knew it. *I know I can't physically stop him now, even if I wanted to, but I should at least make an effort.*

She could do nothing but groan, low pitched and relatively quiet at first, then higher pitched sounds began emanating from her throat with more volume and frequency as the pleasures began to cascade.

After a minute or two of pleasurable waves crashing throughout her body and brain, Rhonda made a last-ditch effort to *not* screw him the first time they met!

"Baby, when you kiss me like that it feels so good I can't stand it! Let me kiss you nicely, too!" grabbing at his crotch for what was surely another big, beautiful muscle.

Great! She wants to give me some head!

Thomas stopped suckling her breast to unzip his dungarees, unwittingly giving her some time to regroup and organize her thoughts, as he rolled onto his back and she fished around in his underwear for perhaps his finest muscle.

Rhonda was very pleased to realize she hadn't lost the oral skills she'd perfected on Marc, even though the only oral sex she had been having for the past six months was a very different kind.

Hot Rod is a trophy fuck and truly fabulous, but I don't want to screw him the first time we meet! I don't see myself as a slut, and only sluts do it on the first date!

So she decided to drain him dry orally but make it last ten minutes so it would be memorable for both of them. Rhonda couldn't wrap her hands around his biceps, even with two hands, and she couldn't wrap her hand entirely around his fat cock, either. *He's bigger than Marc, all the way around. What a fantastic fit its going to be inside me, eventually!*

After her process of inspired caresses, strokes, kisses, licks, and sensual sucking, she felt his finest muscle erupt into her mouth, and sweetly absorbed every drop of him. *The marijuana has relaxed me and somehow given me sensual inspiration! Its my finest cock and strongest ejaculation, ever! This has got to please him. I bet he'll take me for more motorcycle rides after this!*

161

Hot Rod certainly seemed like he enjoyed it. He'd been moaning and groaning, hands in her hair, hips thrusting, throughout the entire performance! *I have the indisputable proof of his satisfaction in my mouth and stomach!*

It was definitely one of the best blow jobs Hot Rod had experienced in a while. Only Peggy, the popular and aptly-named head cheerleader, and Donna Sue, the very pretty and built brunette Southern Homecoming Princess had orally pleased and satisfied his so well. *And I only met this chick an hour ago! Amazing.*

No complications were wanted, on either part, and her smooth swallows solved the disposal problem. *Non-swallowers don't last long in my world,* Hot Rod smugly reminded himself as he watched her. *There are too many who like and enjoy it to put up with unnecessary complications like cleaning up afterward.*

For the time being he was relaxed and satisfied, but Hot Rod was already looking forward to taking her on another ride, and next time he was pretty sure the rest of her other magical treasures would be revealed.

At the beginning of the summer I set a goal to pluck five cherries, and if this girl's a virgin, and I strongly suspect she is, Rhonda'll be the third—and it's only July!

When Rhonda returned, Gwen was waiting at the weightlifting pen, frantic to find her. *My mom will be returning to the beach in less than an hour to pick us up!*

"There you are! Where the hell have you been? Alice told me she saw you riding off on the back of some guy's motorcycle! Did you ride off with Hot Rod? You just met him! What the fuck were you thinking? Are you fucking nuts?!!"

162

Gwen had something of Irish temper, at times.

Rhonda was buzzed, her speech slow and fuzzy. She was both relaxed and hopped up at the same time.

"Turn around so I can check you over and make sure you're okay."

Inspecting Rhonda over from head to toe and finding no obvious cuts, bruises, or physical damage, Gwen relaxed a bit. "I am mainly just glad you're okay." Now that Rhonda was confirmed safe and sound, however, Gwen wanted details.

Asking about where they had gone and what they had done, Rhonda mumbled something about a fast motorcycle ride to a cabin in the woods, a joint, and Hot Rod's joint, with a constant and continuous grin and giggle.

It's pretty obvious Rhonda is buzzed.

"When my mom comes to pick us up, you better pretend you have been sleeping in the sun. Pretend you're asleep all the way home. Don't say a word! Do you hear me? When we get to my house, you're coming with me for a shower and to change clothes. Got that?"

Drifting into a relaxed and deeply satisfied sleep in the car on the way home, Rhonda pretended to still be half-asleep before going into Gwen's room to shower and clean up.

It was almost two hours later before Rhonda could make enough rational sense without giggling and smiling to tell Gwen all about what had happened with Hot Rod.

The same excitement, smile, and sensuality Rhonda had felt with Marc had returned, Gwen noticed.

She is absolutely gushing about Hot Rod, his muscles, his motorcycle, how confident he is, and how he shared his pot with her. Rhonda also effusively reported all about his devil-may-care attitude, the cabin in the woods—where they could be alone together without adults around—and his beautiful cock.

Raving further, she went on for at least ten minutes about the thrill of riding behind him, holding him tight, the smell of his leather jacket, the wind in her hair, cars flashing by, and the warmth of the sun on her face.

It's clear to me that Rhonda has chosen Hot Rod to be her first male lover. A small part of Gwen was initially jealous, but then remembered all the things she had done with Ruben. *And while my Mr. Hirsch is not in the same league as Hot Rod, he is very nice, very intelligent, a nice guy, and likes me a lot.*

Both Rhonda's and Gwen's dads took the family cars to work weekdays, so the only time the girls could go to the beach was on the weekends, when one or the other mom had access to the car and would drive them. They would be dropped off at ten in the morning and picked up at four in the afternoon, usually with their little sisters and some other girls from the neighborhood.

I can hardly wait to meet Hot Rod next Saturday! Calling some other regular Lake Lilly girls, Rhonda found out from them Hot Rod went to the beach every day on his motorcycle, so she was almost positive he would be there. *He is independent and free! Not only that, he has a place to go so we can be alone together, without parents! It's perfect!*

Sure, it was a rundown shack, but it was more than most boys she knew had to offer. Plus, Hot Rod had huge muscles, and pot to relax them, and a motorcycle! *Since Thomas is older and more experienced, I'll bet he'll have a rubber when we need one.*

If he didn't, she would need a good Plan B. *Another blowjob would be okay, but I'm determined to pluck that trophy!*

Hot Rod had everything a sixteen-year-old girl could want. *He has attitude, wheels, beautiful muscles, money, a place to go so we can have sex together, and good pot! What more could I ask for?*

Rhonda, of course, had everything a seventeen-year-old guy could ask for: a nice figure, runaway hormones and natural horniness, and a cherry she anxiously wanted to give away.

Once her mom had finally driven off the next Saturday, Rhonda and Gwen left their little sisters on their towels by the beach and went immediately to the weightlifters area to look for Thomas, both with some excitement and trepidation.

They found him talking and laughing with some guys and girls Rhonda didn't know. *Most of them appear older, probably juniors and seniors at Northside High.*

Hot Rod nodded at Rhonda and Gwen when he saw them, waved, and smiled, holding up ten fingers, indicating he would be over to visit them shortly, so they waited.

Ten minutes later, Rhonda introduced Gwen to him and both girls were trembling with anticipation and excitement, but neither could help herself. Like Rhonda, she found the muscles, power, and machismo to be fascinating! *Intoxicating! I can barely resist the urge to grab a feel of his muscles myself! I can see now what Rhonda was talking about. Whew!*

Gwen's hormones had been stimulated by all of the muscles and testosterone, too, and were also percolating nicely under the surface. *I know if Hot Rod asked me to ride with him, too, sometime, his offer would be accepted in a New York minute!*

That information would be kept to herself, though, as she was thinking with **her** lower brain, right then, and it would certainly complicate things with Rhonda…and Ruben.

The redhead is certainly doable, Hot Rod decided, *but Rhonda is the sweet, young, oh-so-willing prize.*

Thomas was very nice and polite to both girls, flirting just a little before whispering his plans in Rhonda's ear as he turned to leave.

"I have a few people to see first, but be ready to ride around eleven, okay?" smiling at Rhonda until she grinned back.

Nodding to Gwen, Hot Rod smirked and squeezed Rhonda's waist lightly as he left.

Eleven o'clock is perfect, Rhonda thought. *I'll have plenty of time with Thomas, and still enough time for the pot high to wear off before my mom returns to pick us up at four.*

Hot Rod had his plan for her, and she had her plan for him. Fortunately, both plans involved them getting a nice, relaxing buzz on and having incredibly intense, pleasurable, and satisfying sex.

I'm very much hoping and praying he has a rubber!

Much to her relief, and excitement, when they arrived at the cabin, he *did* have a prophylactic.

Now all I have to worry about is whether the rubber will break inside me. The anticipation and excitement was growing.

"You are so strong, Hot Rod! Have you ever broken a rubber?"

"Nope. I use nothing but the best rubbers, Rhonda!"

He insisted it was a remote possibility, when they flopped down on the mattress, but she wasn't as sure.

"Have you ever lost one…inside…you know…or broke?"

"Nope. Once I put it on, it sticks like glue! Don't worry. I am not looking forward to making any babies either!" he assured her, smiling.

Rhonda had mixed feelings.

Part of her—the horny part—was *so* excited! The basic, biological, virginal female portion of her anxiously wanted him inside her, all of him all the way inside, to fill her up and have it done, so she could begin the new phase of her life as a sexually active female, and a potential mate sometime in the future. *I'm looking forward to an energetic, busy, and satisfying sex life, starting with Hot Rod.*

The rational part, on the other hand, was anxious about the rubber, an unknown and untested entity, and its durability. Failure of the rubber to function properly could have serious, life-altering consequences. *I'm not looking forward to being pregnant and a mother anytime soon. I don't even like to think about what my parents would do. They might even send me away to a home for unwed mothers or something!*

In the end, the excitement and anticipation of bagging Hot Rod as her first trophy fuck outweighed the reservations about the durability of the rubber. *The die is cast. It's finally happening!*

While lying naked on the mattress, she took five little puffs on the joint he passed to her. That seemed to be enough to calm most of her fears while she waited for him to get naked, find the rubber, peel it away from the aluminum wrapper, and roll the rubber down his beautifully stiff cock, covering over 80% of the shaft. *Jeez, it's simply beautiful! He's gorgeous! I'm warm and moist already, so ready! Another absolutely fabulous hard-on to my credit! Ding! So that's how a rubber goes on! And he does it; I don't have to do a thing. It looks so simple when he does it!*

The very *thought* of him and his muscles on top of her and between her legs, pinning her to the mattress, his beautiful cock buried deep inside her and plunging repeatedly, safely, and enjoyably, made her tremble with anticipation.

Hot Rod figured that Rhonda seemed pretty willing, so he wasn't too concerned she would protest. *When she didn't resist me while I took her bikini off after a few kisses, I knew there would be no resistance. She wants to screw me, too!* He was prepared for any verbal or physical defenses she might come up with, but all she asked was if he had a dependable rubber!

*I am **in**, literally and figuratively!*

It was pretty easy to tell this was her maiden voyage because she gave him a shy smile and looked away when he removed her bikini completely, crossing her ankles and covering her breasts with one arm and her bush with the other hand.

It feels great to think I'm probably the first guy to see her completely naked. It was to be a full day of firsts.

"Nice," he observed, with an approving smile and a frankly sexual once-over.

Still a bit apprehensive even after taking several tokes on the joint, his positive comments helped her to calm down more. *Hot Rod likes what he sees and his stiff hardon tells me he wants me.*

Thomas was pleased because she was a beauty and he wanted to make sure this wasn't messed up! His stomach tightened a little and his pulse was increasing steadily. *If I screw it up, Rhonda might tell her girlfriends and there might not be any more easy cherries to be plucked anytime soon. The more relaxed she is, the better it will be for both of us.*

Hot Rod was very impressed by her natural good looks, the soft warm slopes, valleys, and bushy uncharted territory. A woody had quickly risen to the occasion. *Hello Woodrow, I'm glad to see you again! We are both in for a treat today!*

She was no less impressed and thrilled with the beauty of his body, too. *I have never seen a guy so muscled and masculine in my life! Oh my God! This is a real man, in every sense of the word. Marc was nice, but he can't compare with this guy. Hot Rod is all man! A young man, to be sure, but as masculine as I could ever hope for!*

Even as he was stroking her breasts, kissing them, and telling her how nice they were, she began caressing his arms, shoulders, and belly in return, gushing about his flexing muscles as the mutual explorations progressed. *The pot has relaxed me somewhat, but I'm still trembling and nervous.*

"You are so big, and strong, and beautiful!" Rhonda heard a voice she later recognized as her own, marveling as her hands tried to wrap around his bicep.

Hot Rod was pleased to hear her groan and moan as he kissed her and lightly stroked her entire body, head to toe, before leaning down to tickle and tease her stiff nipples with his tongue. *Her hips have started to twitch, and I know she's getting wetter and warmer, readying a warm and welcoming reception for me!*

"Ummm..unh!" Rhonda let out a primal groan of pleasure as he slipped a digit inside her soaking femaleness, which almost immediately began grasping and releasing his finger, repeatedly, surrounding and engulfing him in silky warmth, and juicy, wanton need, waiting and wanting to enable a smooth, pleasurable, and very memorable first-entry experience, for both of them, very soon.

I'm very ready to meet what I see as my romantic destiny, physically, sexually, and emotionally, with Hot Rod. His incredibly strong hard-on is undeniable evidence he thinks I'm desirable, sexy, and attractive. His ramrod member makes Hot Rod sexy, and the rubber makes him mostly safe!

Taking his time, Thomas enjoyed stroking her warm and receptive body, making her groan, moan, and writhe with involuntary pleasure, spending another several minutes kissing her mouth, breasts, belly, and working his way down her body, thoroughly pleasing as many of her sensitive and pleasurable spots as possible, groaning with considerable delight along with her as the trail of strategic, warm kisses drifted steadily lower.

I want her first experience to be a good one so she'll let me bang her in the future whenever I'm horny!

Brushing his lips lightly across her stomach and reaching her trimmed bush, he slid across her thigh and between her legs, put his massive arms under her hips, and eventually rested both hands on her lower belly, just above her bush.

Smiling at her from just above the curly pubic hair, he then lowered his gaze to admire her swollen lips, waiting and wanting some attention, before attaching his salivating lips to hers. *She is so juicy, and ready!*

Mm-hmm...tasty, soaking wet....even sweet. This is gonna be gooood! burying his tongue inside her tasty, tiny pink overflowing crease.

Rhonda was in ecstasy. "Oh my God! Does that feel good! Yeah, baby! I love it! Jesus!!!"...*oh...oh yes!...oh Yes!...YES!...*

He licks me as good as Gwen does! I absolutely love *it!*

Her reservations and resistance, the little there were, melted away to puddles of primeval passion.

I do *enjoy driving them crazy,* Hot Rod thought, *but really, bottom line, I also can't* wait *to slide my cock all the way inside her! I want the good stuff!*

170

"Mm…yeah…your pussy tastes good…" murmuring low.

The very thought of any guy, much less Hot Rod, tasting my pussy is thrilling! He thinks I taste good, and is doing it just right! I'm tickled and thrilled to know guys can do it good, too.

In addition, Thomas was not just taking a brief taste, a tease. *I'm keeping on her with my mouth until she absolutely can't stand anymore pleasure!* From experience, he could tell the trembling, intensely pleasurable shockwaves were rapidly intensifying and approaching the undeniable phase.

"Ummm"….low groan…. "Oooohhh!"…higher pitched…. "Unh!"…."oh yes! Yes!!...iiieee!…"

"You taste so good and are so fucking, soaking wet!" he exclaimed in a brief pause, tipping her over the ledge toward her then-inescapable orgasm.

He likes the taste of my pussy! You can eat my pussy all you want, cowboy! Help yourself! Please! Don't stop!

A high-pitched shriek of pure pleasure escaped her throat.

Her hips started to twitch with a mind of their own and Rhonda knew she was in delicious trouble as his tongue flicked and flirted all along the honey trail, top to bottom, bottom to top, spending ten seconds or so at the top, his right hand curling around her hips and massaging her bush and clit, until the intense pleasures building up inside her became irresistible and gave into the impending sensual tsunami. Wave after wave of indescribable pleasure flooded her brain and body until she lost track of where she was and why. *I'm in heaven! It feels like I have left the Earth's surface! Oh no!…Oh yes! Yes! YES!...*

Lapping the sweetness, Thomas continued dipping his tongue inside and drinking from the tiny, two-inch, swollen, overflowing and rhythmically squeezing pink slit until there was no doubt she was in the throes of orgasm, the sign he was waiting for to mount her.

That'll give her something to tell her girlfriends about. Free advertising! Life just keeps getting better!

Rhonda was very glad she had showered earlier in the morning and taken special care with her hygiene, although in her wildest dreams she had never anticipated this! *He likes the taste of me! Holy crap! I can't believe it! Fuck me!!! Yes! Fuck me now!*

Once she'd had her loud, shuddering, groaning, trembling orgasm, Hot Rod knew there was no way she could refuse him his relief! *Her surrender will be complete! It's my turn to receive.*

Rhonda had never experienced that relaxing and complete an orgasm before! *If that's just the foreplay, I can't even imagine how fucking fabulous the rest is gonna be! The promise of an even more sensual, penetrating, and very different pleasurable treats awaiting me, bringing exciting new potentials with it, make it unique and incredibly special.*

Thomas was pretty satisfied with himself as he watched her stop quivering and trembling, her muscles relaxing, eyes opening a little and starting to focus again, her juiciness subsiding slightly, not overflowing, just maintaining a wet, warm, and willing state of readiness.

I almost always tongue the virgins to overcome any residual resistance they may have and make my entry so much easier and more pleasurable for both of us. After screwing them the first couple times, I don't have to taste them for them to give it up, so I usually don't, but she knows what I can do, if I want, so it's usually better to keep them hoping.

Having her as juicy and wanting as possible beforehand was his goal for every girl, so he would usually give them a couple lingual strokes before hopping into the saddle.

I've given, so now it's my turn to receive.

Feeling his thick, powerful arms under her knees, her legs in the air, and his large, tanned hands at her sides, Rhonda gradually became aware of the tip of his cock slowly pushing against her swollen, engorged labia as he mounted and gradually eased his way inside her.

I can't decide whether to close my eyes so I can better feel him penetrating me or keep them open to watch him disappearing inside me! I wish I could do both! She decided to close her eyes to focus and more intensely enjoy the once-in-a-lifetime feel of her first real, male lover fully sliding inside her!

He's in me! Then she felt more than a twinge of pain as he slid in farther, inch by inch, until Hot Rod was almost all the way in. *Its done! His muscular, ripped, hard belly is flush with mine on each stroke. I'm now a full-fledged woman!*

A new chapter in her life had started, and she was absolutely thrilled to realize it. *The* thought *of a guy like Hot Rod all the way inside me is amazing, and the reality is even better!*

When Hot Rod began to feel some resistance, he paused a couple seconds to let her shift her hips a little to prepare herself for the final plunge, and then resumed easing himself deeper until the resistance faded to nothing and he was all the way home.

I saw her wince a couple times as I sank slowly but steadily deeper inside, pausing briefly along the way, until the resistance subsided, and then disappeared. A satisfied grin appeared on Rhonda's face and she relaxed, gently but firmly receiving, accepting, and gladly gripping his every stroke, her lower lady lips tightening and relaxing, caressing and stroking him gently but firmly with each thrust.

Je-sus! Is she tight! Silky soft! Warm! And wet!

The thought of him all the way inside her was almost as satisfying as the thrust itself. *I'm actually Doing It with the most popular, muscular, and coolest guy at the entire beach! There's no doubt now whether he finds me attractive and sexy!*

Hooking her heels on either side of his hips she tried to pull him in further with each thrust, wanting all of him as deep inside as possible!

"Yeah, baby! You feel *so* good! I want all of you in me!"

Putting both her hands on his massive arms and chest, Rhonda tried to feel the rest of his muscles, too. *I don't know how long intercourse should or could take, but I'm determined to enjoy the experience to the end! I have heard each guy and each time will be different.* Although she suspected there would be considerable soreness afterward, her hope was it would last long enough for him to have a thoroughly satisfying experience with her.

I wonder if Hot Rod is enjoying me as much as I'm enjoying him. His eyes are closed and he's moaning and groaning with almost every stroke, right along with me, so I hope he is!

Several extremely pleasurable minutes, and several hundred deep and incredibly pleasurable strokes firmly given and gladly received, had transpired when Hot Rod stiffened, groaned the deep I'm-going to-come-now sound Rhonda was learning to recognize, buried himself deep inside her with a powerful last thrust, and shot his load. She was overjoyed, for both of them, as a sexual couple.

The thought of popping another tight, sexy, warm, willing cherry was incredibly exciting to Hot Rod. *Pussy in general, and getting laid specifically, is pretty amazing, but to be the first one to bang her is something else. Rhonda is so tight, warm, and juicy—and is fucking me back! She'll never forget me, now. I'm her first.*

Thomas would also never forget her, either.

Most conquests are unforgettable, his and hers.

Rhonda had pleased and satisfied him, which pleased and satisfied her. Knowing she'd had Hot Rod's cock and semen deep inside her, but was probably safe if the rubber worked properly, was incredibly satisfying to know.

What a freakin' fabulous fit!

She had thoroughly enjoyed herself, immensely even, but was worried about having more orgasms with him deep inside her because she'd heard having an orgasm with him increased the chances of getting pregnant, if the rubber broke.

For that reason, Rhonda hoped the rubber was intact, mainly because it wasn't possible for her to stop coming, even if she had wanted to, which she didn't.

Having one orgasm first, orally, before Thomas entered me, was incredibly nice, too, although letting him know he can also make me orally cum makes me vulnerable, too. I lost my sexual leverage, but I don't really care because it was worth it!

Rhonda knew how the guys felt after she had suckled them to orgasm: pleased, relaxed, and satisfied, but a little vulnerable. *Hot Rod has tasted me to orgasm, too, and it can be done again, if he wants, just like I can do it with the guys whenever the spirit moves me.* It was a pleasant awakening. The sexual scales were now more balanced.

The pleasure and satisfaction of the moment overrode the possible broken rubber vulnerability concern, and Rhonda just decided to enjoy it for what it was—a purely satisfying, unique, once-in-a-lifetime personal pleasure. *My romantic future is fucking fabulous!*

To start off her sexual career with a trophy fuck like Hot Rod was fantastic. Both had thoroughly enjoyed themselves and were basking in the relaxing afterglow of incredibly satisfying orgasms.

When Hot Rod collapsed on her, she couldn't move to find the rubber because his almost two hundred pounds of muscle were dead weight and too much for Rhonda to move. *Its impossible for me to fully relax and enjoy the moment until I am sure the condom is intact.*

Waiting until he nodded off to sleep and slid off to the left side of her, she scooted out from underneath him and freed herself to search for the rubber.

There it is!

Quickly finding it, intact, Rhonda smelled it quickly and happily slipped it into a sealable baggie in her purse, full of him, upright, so it wouldn't spill, for later enjoyment and sharing.

Then, and not until then, was she able to fully relax and enjoy what had just happened. *I am relaxed, excited, pleased, proud, more than a little sore, and very satisfied, all at the same time!*

Hot Rod had tasted pussy before, Rhonda could tell, by his confidence and technique in going down on her, and for a few seconds she was a little jealous of those other girls. *At the same time, I'm glad he is older and more experienced. Damn, it felt*

176

fucking great! Fabulous! Hot Rod can eat my pussy all he wants!

Additionally, the thought of him all the way inside her, filling her with his cock and cum, was almost as satisfying as the slow entrance and gradually deeper thrusting itself. It was another fine step in her sexual awakening and education.

Everything is perfect.

Hot Rod didn't really notice how she was doing after he had entered her the whole way, breaking through her virginal barrier, because of her soaking wetness when he first mounted her. *There's no doubt she's incredibly ready to be entered and is enjoying it and looking forward to it, maybe as much as I am!*

Besides, once he had entered her, waves of amazingly warm pleasure were spreading throughout his body, short-circuiting his thinking processes, and leaving him on a hip-thrusting, penile pleasure-seeking, primeval automatic pilot.

There was also no doubt in his mind Rhonda had already experienced a tasty orgasm prior to mounting her, and she was screwing him back vigorously, moaning and groaning, eyes closed, hips bouncing and lower lips grasping and releasing him in a warm, welcoming wetness, a velvet kiss and caress on each stroke, once he was securely inside her.

From my prior experience, I'm pretty sure the sex was mutually pleasurable and satisfying. Once Thomas let it go, he had drifted off into a relaxing and incredibly satisfying sleep.

Mission accomplished—for both of us.

The possibility the rubber might break never really crossed his mind while in mid-stroke, but Hot Rod did give it a quick, satisfied glance when he was done, as it appeared to be unbroken on his rapidly wilting shaft, before he slid to the side and nodded off to sleep.

Good quality, brand-name rubbers are all he used, on advice from his good friend Howie, who also bought them for him.

I'm glad she didn't bleed very much, though, or I'd have had a real mess on this mattress.

There was no indoor plumbing at the cabin, just an old, smelly, dilapidated outhouse out back, but Rhonda found some toilet paper on a small beat-up shelf on the back wall and cleaned the small amount of blood, maybe a thimble-full, from dripping down her thighs, and then lay back down on the mattress next to him, hugging him and feeling very close to him.

Although a little raw and aching, Rhonda was already wondering when they could do it again. *I'm sure each time will just continue getting better and better! I wonder if he has another rubber! I hope so!*

A quiet tear ran down Rhonda's cheek and across his chest but she didn't really cry or sob because there was much more happiness than sadness inside. It was a tear for what had been lost in the process of becoming a woman. Something important had been lost, and something equally important had been gained.

Hot Rod was particularly glad she didn't cry afterward because it would just complicate things by adding in too much emotion. *This is just friendly fucking. I don't plan on getting emotionally wrapped up in her.*

Two other girls had cried after he'd deflowered them. Bobbi first, a cute and surprisingly bosomy dirty-blond, Honor Roll student who wanted one day to be a veterinarian to help save abused animals, and then Janine two weeks later, with her knockout figure and bikini, fine ass, and reputation for only allowing oral sex and sixty-nine before Hot Rod persuaded her to give it up.

Thomas felt bad for a while, a little guilty, like he had stolen something from them. Thinking again, he thought, *I've only taken what they were naturally going to give away to somebody anyway, eventually. It might as well be me! None of them were forced. Sure, I gave them pot, but they could have refused. It isn't rape! It is consensual sex. Screwing. Friendly fucking. Call it what you want. If they are going to eventually give their pussy away to somebody,* and they are, *they could do a lot worse than to give it to me!*

And Hot Rod *did* like them; he liked *all* of them.

I like screwing all of them, but I don't like the emotional baggage and weight they bring with them. After an hour of thought and rationalization, he convinced himself it was okay to bang as many as possible because *they know from the start I'm a bad boy! They should know better than to expect romance, hand holding, and true love from me. It just isn't my style. I see myself definitely as a stud, and a stud services* all *the fillies!*

So, once the dirty deed was done, and after the tears, he decided to not give either Bobbi or Janine anymore rides on his motorcycle, or otherwise.

Getting too attached to any one female can limit my opportunities with all the other girls, and I don't want any limitations on me. Thomas had put in a lot of sweat and hard work to get in this position, and now the hard work was coming to fruition he wanted to enjoy it completely. To him, there were just too many fish in the sea waiting to be snagged.

Hot Rod spent six months the summer before his junior year sculpting his body from head to toe with hundreds of pushups, thousands of sit-ups, and weightlifting a couple hours or so every day to make up for his otherwise fairly average facial looks.

The motorcycle, bad attitude, and the money from his pot sales added to his rebel persona, and he knew it. *The girls are offering their special gifts, and I'm offering mine. I'm an Alpha Male, plain and simple.*

It is theorized a guy reaches his sexual peak at eighteen years old, and Thomas would be eighteen soon. The hormones were also running wild on the female side of the sexual fence, and he was determined to make the most of both of those biological details.

At the time, however, Rhonda didn't know anything about Hot Rod's decision to enjoy any and all the wild and willing, wanton pussy. *I heard he was pretty popular with the girls and played the field in the past, but I think it's just because none of the other girls had to offer what I am offering!* It made him a challenge.

If Rhonda was brutally honest with herself, she would have to admit having sex with several of her attractive classmates sounded like a pretty good idea, too. Thomas was not the only teen who brought her runaway hormones to a boil! *He'll just be the first!* She did plan to be somewhat discrete and careful about it, though.

Even though Hot Rod is not the only one on my to-do list of potential sex partners, he's near the very top, if not at the very top!

And if she could actually become his girlfriend, that would be her crowning accomplishment and seriously enhance her standing with the other girls, while boosting her self-esteem.

Hot Rod never noticed the rubber was missing when he woke up thirty minutes later, and Rhonda wasn't going to mention it. Disappointed when he kissed her on the forehead and told her to get dressed, instead of rolling on top of her and putting it back in again, she said nothing.

Maybe he doesn't have another clean rubber. Maybe I just took all of his energy—that's it! She much preferred the latter thought to the others, and there was a lot of truth in her belief.

In any case, its a roaring success! Hot Rod and I are fuck buddies, at least. Maybe I will eventually become his girlfriend!

Hot Rod's used rubber was shared with Gwen at home, letting her smell it, but not taste it, because it was very special now.

Besides, Gwen had Ruben now, and no real need for anyone else's leftover semen.

For the next month, Rhonda was Hot Rod's Saturday biker babe, going off with him for two or three hours each time and returning in time for their ride home, buzzed and relaxed, but not really spacy or too obviously stoned.

It made her smile to herself when other girls jealously watched. *Out of all the girls, even the older girls, who routinely tried to get his attention and failed, I've succeeded. I'm The Chosen One!* Her sexual and social confidence soared. *He's a real prize! Rack up one for The Liberated Woman! I screw who I want.*

Gwen would worry about Rhonda each time she roared off with Hot Rod, but there was very little to be said or done about it. She had made her mind up.

Alice and Patricia were also at the beach every time Rhonda went off with Hot Rod. Both little sisters were sworn to secrecy, with Rhonda and Gwen promising them they wouldn't tell on *them* when *they* wanted time alone with their own boyfriends someday soon.

Rhonda learned a lot about Hot Rod in the next month. For instance, he spent most of his time at the cabin rather than at his parents' house. With no running water there, he never bathed much, and preferred to jump in the lake a couple times a day to wash off the sweat.

Lifting weights for hours at Lake Lilly was hard, dirty, and sweaty exercise, as was roaring around town on his motorcycle, shirtless or with muscle shirts with the sleeves torn off, in the scorching summer sun, but he didn't notice or care. Thomas was a physically imposing figure with or without his shirt and was more interested in how he looked than his odor.

Deodorants and soap are for pussies who want to smell good. Not me! Take me as I am, naturally, or don't take me at all. When it got too bad, to the point where he could smell himself, Hot Rod would jump in the lake, but without soap.

I like the smell of Thomas' sweat to an extent, but after some hot, summer days in the nineties, its just dripping off him everywhere, frequently on me. Hot Rod could have used a shower, or at least some deodorant, but he didn't appear to notice, or care, so she didn't say anything. Every three or four days, he shaved.

The cabin wasn't air-conditioned, of course, so on those really hot days, even a few minutes of serious screwing would leave both of them covered in sweat, his and hers. *It isn't a big problem for me though, because I mostly see it as romantic, sexy sweat.*

Rhonda enjoyed just being with him, riding his motorcycle fast in the sun and the wind together, squeezing his waist tight and holding on as he popped wheelies or ran stop signs, and feeling his massive muscles on top of and in her. *Life is good! Why rock the boat? A little sweat is nothing!*

Pot was clearly something that enhanced the sexual experience, mainly because it helped her to relax and drift off into a dreamy state, like she was floating, where every touch was electric, exciting, and pleasurable. *My usual inhibitions just melt away. Its amazing how much pleasure and satisfaction I can give and receive when I'm more relaxed.*

Comparing and contrasting Marc and Hot Rod, and her experiences with each, there were obvious physical differences, with Hot Rod being older, more masculine, and more muscularly well defined, and just bigger—all over.

The main similarity in Marc and Hot Rod was their lack of emotional sharing and closeness after they were finished. Marc and Hot Rod were exhausted afterward, drowsy, and unable and/or unwilling to share.

Doubt began to creep into her head regarding whether *any* guy was capable of the type of emotional closeness she had experienced with Gwen after sex. If the two guys she had been with so far were any indication, it didn't give her much hope for finding one who was.

Pleasing and satisfying guys is great, but I want and need pillow talk, some affection, an appreciation, and a reassurance I am sexy, desirable, and satisfying, along with an emotional closeness, sharing, and bonding.

Eventually, Rhonda asked Hot Rod to come to her house and pick her up on his motorcycle even though she was pretty sure her mom would refuse to allow it to happen. To Teresa, motorcycles were loud, dirty, and dusty, and usually driven too fast and irresponsibly by scruffy, rowdy, daredevils, Wesley included!

Thomas is an older guy, his nickname is Hot Rod, and he's a biker, so those are three strikes against him right off the bat! Her mom's fear was of all things associated with motorcycles and the bikers who rode them, so she certainly wasn't going to allow her daughter to ride off with a biker. *No way.*

Hot Rod had no interest in picking her up at her house or meeting her family, so he made excuses. *Meeting her family is for serious daters. We are just having seriously satisfying sex.*

Rhonda was testing him to see what other things he would do for her. Home pick-up? Meeting the family? No. Rubber? Yes.

Over the next couple weeks, it soon became pretty clear to Rhonda Thomas was making excuses to get out of picking her up at her home, saying he had people to meet and important things to do. *I know what he means, vaguely, but am hoping Thomas thinks of me as one of those important people and things to do, too.*

One Saturday, Rhonda had just started her period the day before so she relieved him orally at the cabin. He came like a volcanic eruption, and she was glad to ingest and absorb every drop. Seeing and feeling him ejaculate pleased her, and wasn't possible when he was inside her, especially with the rubber on. As with Marc, she was visually stimulated by watching a large spurt or two arc in her direction and splash on her skin. *Shooting a large load is a good sign to me,* she thought, *because it is a fairly good indication he has saved it for me!* She *hoped* he had saved it for her, at least, but she *did* have some nagging doubts.

There was also something satisfying about a strong spurt into her face because it meant she was getting all of it and there would be less oozing afterward to be coaxed out of him. *I gauge his passion, desire, and want for me by the force of his ejaculation.*

His semen is a little different than Marc's but tastes just as good, maybe even better. I'm getting a little better at giving head every time. Progress!

Admiring his muscularity after sex, Rhonda often caressed and kissed his arms, shoulders, and belly while he dozed off to sleep, finally resting her head on his belly, drifting off to a light but satisfied sleep as well.

Gwen was concerned when they returned after only an hour on that Saturday Rhonda had only given him a blow job, afraid they had an argument or something. Rhonda calmed her fears with a quick explanation about the unfortunate biological timing. Anal penetration had been the other offer, but he had declined and rolled onto his back to facilitate her oral efforts.

Massaging his balls gently as she pleasured him was another first for her, even taking them into her mouth and sucking them gently, with his direction. *It pleases me when he tells me various ways to pleasure him because I want to learn all the possible ways to do it, and I particularly like when Hot Rod takes control. There is just something animal... or dominant... something... about it.*

During the week she invested in two new, particularly fetching bikinis, a tiny white one and a smaller pink one—and by Saturday Rhonda was as hot as a pistol, practically tearing Hot Rod's clothes off as soon as they got inside the cabin!

As luck would have it, he didn't have a rubber that day. They quickly agreed he would stay inside her until he felt his load ready to explode and would then pull it out and ejaculate into her mouth. *Safe intercourse!* Rhonda mistakenly thought. She was unaware that it could possibly impregnate her even from his pre-cum fluids.

There was no need for Hot Rod to orally prepare her that day. He knew there was a honey pot of swollen, way overdue, and overflowing passion gurgling just below the boiling point, waiting for him to ignite. *She isn't going to be denied!*

Rhonda's first sexual intercourse without a rubber held for her a thrill similar to what she thought skydiving must be like: it was exciting because she could really feel him inside her, could feel every twinge of his muscle, with nothing between them; but it was incredibly scary to think that one wrong move, one bit of delay could easily change the course of her life.

Part of her was wanting, needing, and begging for him to plant his cock and empty his seed deep inside her! The rational part resisted the primeval urge. *The thought of him planting his seed deep inside me feels very natural, but the potential consequences are scary!* Ultimately she wanted him all the way inside her, barrier-free, filling her with cock and cum, and being on The Pill would allow it to safely happen. *Until then, a high-quality rubber will have to do.*

Ten furious, fucking moments later, her frequent wailings, yelps, squeals, groans, shrieks, and helpless whimpering as he nailed her to the mattress and probed her pussy in every possible manner, accelerated his excitement and pleasure, moving him closer to his ultimate release.

Rhonda was horny as a goat and thoroughly enjoying the fucking!

"Oh! God yes, baby! Right *there!*" Small, almost imperceptible shifts in her hips from stroke to stroke would guide him exactly where she wanted him to be.

"Ieeeee!...Unh! Ieee! Oh, baby!"

Her passion, excitement, and reciprocity turned him on, and the sex was fast and furious. As he felt his load starting to approach his own boiling point, he took control.

"Put your legs straight down! Now! Flat!"

"Oh yeah baby…are you ready to cum? Give it to me!"

Once her legs were flat he moved from between them to a straddle position with his knees on either side of her thighs, but his cock still inside her.

"Just a couple more strokes…" he groaned, and buried himself once again…deeply and completely…

The pleasurable-seeking, biological side of my brain is dying to drive myself deep inside her silky, warm, drenched honey slit, which is sucking me still deeper, sweeter, and stronger!

"Oh, baby! Give it all to me! Now! I want it! Please!"

She wants it deep, too!

He would be totally surrounding himself with a little bit of warm, welcoming tunnel of silky heaven whose natural urge was to draw him deeper, exactly what he wanted. *Shooting my load deep inside her, burying every possible inch of me inside her velvet softness would be the most naturally satisfying dream I could hope for! What could be better!*

"Yeah baby! Here it comes…"

I love it when Thomas calls me baby.

Yes, the animalistic, instinctual part of his brain *much* preferred driving her home, surrounding his cock with wanton, willing womanliness and planting his seed where no other guy had ever been. *This is some of the best pussy I have ever had! Planting my seed deep within her is so natural, and so tempting I'm fighting my own natural biological, but irrational, impulses!*

The soft, warm, juicy sexiness of her femininity made it very difficult, almost impossible, for him to abruptly withdraw and change course and direction at the very last moment! *She is like silk! Warm, welcoming, velvety, juicy sucking silk!*

187

"Oh yeah, baby!" as he felt the spasm gurgle and start to tingle in his nuts...

At the same time, the rational part of his brain warned him about the real possibility of knocking her up: *Don't do it!*

It was a tossup between the two urges competing in his brain. Fortunately, the very real, rational fear of impregnating her prevailed over the need and satisfaction of planting his seed.

At the very last millisecond he was able to *will* himself out of his natural desire and inclination to finish inside her. Instead, he pulled it out and changed course to another set of also soft, warm, wet, and waiting lips.

"Open your mouth wide. *Now!* Put your tongue out!" he demanded as he took those last four oh-so-pleasing, final, deep silky strokes before blast off, **very** reluctantly withdrew, groaned, and grasping his cock at the base in his right hand, crawled up on his knees toward her outstretched sexy, pink tongue, spraying fresh warm moist jizz in her general direction the entire way!

Rhonda raised her head up to face him and did as she was told. Her mouth open and waiting, she was looking forward to watching him ejaculate. At first her eyes were closed completely, and then opened them to narrow slits, as she didn't want him to squirt into her eyes but did want to see it shoot.

Most importantly, I want to see all three spurts so I can be pretty sure he has withdrawn in time! Three was the magic number, as far as she knew, followed by some oozing, although four or more might be possible. *More cock and more cum is better, almost always, unless it's inside me without a rubber.*

The first strong, warm, squirt from him shot from her waist level as Hot Rod crawled higher on his hands and knees. It was too high and sprayed across her forehead and into her hair. Rhonda flinched reflexively.

188

A millisecond later, the second shot was an over correction to the downside as Thomas crawled even with her breasts and splattered sticky, wet warmth onto her chin and left cheek. By now, Rhonda was welcoming the warm gooey stuff all over her and enjoying the fireworks through narrowed eyes.

His furious crawl reached her head by the time the third shot erupted. Putting the tip of his cock close to the tip of her outstretched pink tongue he sprayed sperm across her tongue, mouth, and nose! *Jizz is flying everywhere!*

Rhonda was glad to count three, large spurts. *I really hope that means he pulled out in time!*

It was truly an amazing afternoon! Rhonda was in no rush to clean herself, and did not resist when Hot Rod used the tip of his wilting cock to smear it all over her face. It was a sperm mask, also her first, and she wanted to literally soak him in for a while, taste, feel, and smell it, both the romantic thought and the actuality. *He pulled it out and came in my face out of consideration for me!*

His reluctantly effective withdrawal had insured, in Rhonda's mind, she was safe from pregnancy while still being sure every drop was hers. *He's protecting me, is worried about me, and respects my fears and feelings. We're thinking alike, a team, working together to maximize our pleasure while minimizing our risk. Maybe we are even a couple!*

A couple girls in Thomas' past hadn't liked the facial at all, because it did make a mess, but Rhonda appeared to accept it in the accommodating and friendly spirit in which it was given.

It further pleased him when she began licking, kissing, and suckling his cock to drain and clean it before starting to lick her lips and clean herself! *Yes! It just feels like the right thing to do!*

Rhonda was learning a new, somewhat risky, alternative birth-control method, and a new taste too: his juices and hers, delightfully mixed together.

The taste of my natural honey nectar combined with his sperm-filled essence is exquisite. It's the best of both worlds!

In return for Rhonda not complaining about or resisting the facial, Thomas scraped some of the sperm off her chin and cheeks with his forefinger and fed it into her mouth as she was licking her lips, a gesture she appreciated. *He wants me to have all of him, too. What a lovely and pleasant thought! He's cleaning me!*

Hot Rod was a willing teacher, and Rhonda was his willing student. There was much to enjoy and learn, for both of them.

Another thing she learned about him was he kept his money and pot in a small eight-by-fifteen-inch storage compartment under the seat of his motorcycle. Thomas would ask her who the stoners, or pot smokers, were at her school and had her introduce them to him. The stoners were glad to have another source of pot, in case their primary source got busted or something. Rhonda was definitely good for his business, and she was glad to be of help.

The pot was rolled up in clear, plastic sandwich baggies to the size of a fat cigar and usually placed in a small brown paper sandwich bag, as well. Rhonda would sometimes deliver a roll in a paper bag to a stoner from her school, put the money in the bag, and return it to Hot Rod.

I am helping Thomas and my friends.

One Saturday she saw a brown paper bag in his storage compartment with what looked like a short pistol barrel sticking out, which made her stomach tighten and pulse flicker. Peeking inside the bag later in the day, she confirmed it was indeed a pistol. *A revolver?*

When she tentatively asked him about the gun and whether it was loaded, he was curt. "Mind your own business!…I have to protect myself against guys who might rob me with a gun or a knife. Don't touch it, 'cause I *always* have it loaded."

It was the beginning of the end for Rhonda and Hot Rod. *Guns scare me. Hunting guns and rifles are one thing. Loaded pistols really scare me because they kill people. Unloaded guns can scare someone, maybe, and might be okay, but loaded guns and the guys who carry them are serious, and not in my future.*

There was a thin line between exciting and just downright dangerous, for Rhonda, and Hot Rod had just crossed over to the seriously scary side of life.

When she learned from the other girls for sure Hot Rod also had different babes for each of the days she wasn't there, and gave each of them rides which also lasted two to three hours, too, it was the final straw! *I am done with him! That SOB! He used me!*

Which was true, of course, but she had also used him.

Rhonda continued going to the beach on Saturdays with the neighborhood girls but stopped hanging around the weightlifting pen so much and gradually tapered her way out of Thomas's life.

Eventually noticing Rhonda wasn't coming around much on Saturdays anymore, Hot Rod didn't really care much because she was starting to get nosy and there were plenty of cuties available to him. *She served her purpose and helped expand my business with the stoners at her school. I'll miss her a little.*

Hot Rod's life took a turn for the worst later that summer when one of his biker babes, Rosita, got jealous of his other females and spread the word around she was late with her period, very late. It wasn't true, of course, but it served Rosita's purpose, and his stable of willing fillies dried up quickly for a couple months.

When, after a couple months, it became obvious Rosita was not pregnant, Hot Rod quickly re-established himself and his previous, pleasurable lifestyle.

Thomas had a very busy and satisfying life for the next five years or so. At nineteen he joined The Avengers motorcycle gang and at age twenty-five was killed in a shoot-out when a gang drug deal went bad.

The six forty-five caliber bullets which tore thru his body at close range had no respect or concern about his muscles, bad attitude, lack of fear, or motorcycle gang membership.

Chapter Twenty-Nine

"College is oh-so-tempting because I have heard they have some wild and crazy fraternity and sorority parties!" Rhonda told Gwen with a laugh midway through her junior year of high school.

But after giving it some serious consideration the first semester of her senior year, she decided it would be easier to capture a guy as a mate who had put the time and energy into a college education and enjoy the benefits of his efforts without ever having attended herself.

"A smart, edgy, ambitious, good-looking, well hung, fun-loving-yet-dependable college graduate who owns and rides a motorcycle and has a good career is Plan A, Gwen!" Rhonda stated with a lot of confidence, like it was a forgone conclusion she could attract a guy like that.

"Plan B is a reliable, blue-collar, middle-to-upper-middle-class party dude with a good job, some basic interests in common, some edge, and a solid future."

It was clear to Gwen Rhonda had given her plans considerable thought.

"Plan C is to attend college myself. I have no idea what I might study, though, and it requires a lot of boring book study, in addition to costing a lot, so it is my plan of last resort. On the positive side, they have some wild parties!" Rhonda added.

"With luck, I might find the best of both worlds—a nice-looking, edgy, ambitious, well-built guy with an education, a good job, and a promising career!" Rhonda confided in Gwen, with a big smile. "A leather jacket and a fast bike would definitely cinch the deal."

My plan is in place! All I need is to find a suitable costar.

Hearing Rhonda's life plan, Gwen smiled. *Its good to have a plan. My plan is also in place, just different.*

It was clear to Gwen college would be her future after high school, with advanced chemistry or biochemistry studies in one of the sciences in graduate school, or maybe even medical school.

During Gwen's senior year, her favorite grandmother, Kate, was diagnosed with breast cancer and died a year later. Gwen decided then she would devote her adult life to becoming a cancer research scientist.

My choices will be in which field of cancer research I will major and at which school. Will it be Diagnostics to find the problem early? Or will it be in developing a treatment or a new miracle drug for a cure? Breast cancer? Brain cancer? Lung cancer? The options were many and the challenge was daunting, but she welcomed it. *It'll be a worthy quest.*

Gwen was looking forward to college because she was smart and had excelled from first grade at academics. *My hope is my academic excellence will earn me one or more scholarships or grants, enough to pay most if not all of my expenses.*

Her main focus in college would be her studies, as Gwen had always reveled in the academic learning process. She would accept the daunting challenge of a cancer research, soaking it all in as she usually did and focusing on her mission.

I'm also interested in meeting people, having a good time, and eventually finding a mate, like Rhonda, but it won't be my main focus. Ruben has given me some confidence in my ability to attract male attention and keep it, and I have a lot of confidence in my academic abilities.

At the same time, Gwen understood Rhonda was mainly interested in learning about and enjoying people, and her studies, if she attended college at all, would always be a secondary interest. *Rhonda might be on a mission if she attends college, but it won't be an academic one.*

It was just two different paths for two similar, but different, girls.

"Do you remember a couple weeks ago when we were discussing our life plans and I told you I wanted to find a successful guy with an excellent future, Gwen? Well, now I know where to find him! The Playboy Mansion is three hours away in Chicago! It's filled with famous actors, musicians, athletes, politicians...you name it! You get to wear those cute Bunny outfits with the Bunny tail and live at The Mansion! It's perfect!"

Gwen was at her practical best. "Oh yeah? First, you have to be twenty-one to serve drinks. And if you research it some more you will see that Bunnies are Strictly Forbidden from dating the customers!"

"Is that right, Gwen? Damn! That would take all the fun out of it!"

Chapter Thirty

Saying goodbye to Gwen when she left for college was a very emotional experience for Rhonda. Their farewell was painful and sad for them because each would miss her BFF terribly!

"Baby, I am going to miss you *so* bad! You are my best and closest girlfriend. My life will never be the same!"

"Me, too, Rhonda! I don't know what I'll do without you!"

Tears were shed, and the fond farewell hugs and kisses lasted well into the night.

"It would be even worse if I thought I would never see you again! But I will call every week and look forward to seeing you at Christmas, spring break, and in the summer! I love you, baby!"

Winning an academic scholarship to a school which was nationally known for its academic and scientific rigor and post-graduate cancer research in Massachusetts, Gwen was ecstatic.

Rhonda had mixed feelings. *I'm sad for myself because my best friend will no longer be next door and readily available whenever I need her. At the same time, I'm happy for Gwen because academic success and cancer research are her goals in*

196

life, something she looks forward to with great excitement and anticipation. I am excited for her!

Saying goodbye after high school graduation was even more difficult for Gwen because it meant bidding farewell to both Ruben and Rhonda. On her porch after their last date with him, the parting was poignant and painful.

"I am so happy for you, Ruben, because you are getting exactly what you want! You are my first and best boyfriend! I love you, and will never forget you. I will miss you like crazy! Thanks for making my life better. For everything! I just know you will be a great astronomer!" Tears freely rolled down her cheeks.

"Gwen, I'm the one who should be thanking *you* for everything. Without you, I don't know where I would be! I love you for everything you are and all you have done for me. I hope you get everything in life you want, because you are a good woman and deserve it!" He hadn't cried in years, since his dad died, but now his hanky was soaked with both of their sweet sadness.

They held each other tight on her front porch for over an hour, neither wanting to ever let go, until Shirley turned the porch light on and came outside, gently telling Gwen to wrap it up.

Ruben had become Gwen's first real boyfriend. Accepted at The University of Chicago, he would excel academically, move on to become a nationally known astrophysicist, marry a colleague, have two kids, and retain fond memories of Gwen his entire life.

There will always be a special place in my heart for Ruben, similar to Rhonda. Gwen was sad to be leaving, but also excited and happy to be moving on toward her life goals. *Rhonda and I will* always *be BFFs and Ruben will always be my first love!*

Rhonda was sad and depressed for two months after Gwen left but then rallied and got a job at a local supermarket as a checkout girl. *I enjoy meeting and interacting with the shoppers, even flirting a little with those hot college guys buying beer!*

When her BFF came home during the Christmas holidays, spring break, and summer vacation, it was like Gwen had never left. They kept in touch by telephone once a week and those giggling, excited campus calls could last for hours!

During her junior and senior years of college, Gwen didn't come home in the summer because she got a chance to work in a lab as an assistant, making a few extra bucks and actually doing basic cancer research.

As Rhonda continued to work, she saved up enough money to buy a jalopy for transportation for $300 from Mario, a guy she knew casually from school, and whose dad owned Roselli's Garage. Mario had worked all his life with his dad and was an excellent mechanic, not to mention a horn dog.

Fixing up old -but-serviceable vehicles and selling them cheap was his sideline. Mario wanted four hundred bucks for the eight-year-old Ford sedan, but Rhonda used her womanly wiles to get it for a hundred less. It was constantly breaking down, however, requiring several more bartering exchanges of services to fix the carburetor and radio, replace the alternator, re-attach the bumper, replace the radiator hose, etc. Over time, he would become quite popular with a half dozen young women of limited financial means but abundant assets. *There are serious fringe benefits to being a mechanic!*

The money at the supermarket was lousy, though, so after twenty months at the supermarket, when a job waitressing at a popular local diner came available Rhonda jumped at it.

An upgrade! Meeting and serving the dining customers is very enjoyable and it is possible to earn a hundred dollars a day in tips, if I hustle! Life was better, but still not good enough to move away from home.

Rhonda traded in her jalopy for a red, three-year-old, sporty Camaro convertible and could be seen all over town zipping here and there. Her lead foot, however, also attracted police attention. After dazzling and flirting her way out of tickets a dozen times with mysteriously unbuttoned blouses, crotch glances, sexy smiles, and high-rise mini-skirts, she ran into a lady cop who was not impressed, dazzled, or interested. Two speeding tickets in the first seven months more than doubled her car-insurance rates, requiring over half of her weekly take-home wages. *Damn!*

"One of the older girls I took judo with, Sandra, is a stewardess, works in New York, and loves it, Gwen! I read a book about it, Coffee, Tea, or Me, about two stews who travel all over the United States and Europe, meeting all kinds of famous movie stars, business executives, and musicians, and getting to know some of them pretty well! It sounds like my kind of fun! And college isn't required!"

"Most good jobs require a college education, you know, Rhonda."

"I know…My mom wants me to stay local and become a teacher, like her, but it requires college and I want to see the world! Travel everywhere! Meet interesting rich and famous people!"

As a liberated woman, I can have any career I want!

After three hard years of waitressing, Rhonda saw a Help Wanted ad recruiting stewardesses for Eastern Airlines in the newspaper. Waitressing was tough work and the new job was promising over twenty thousand a year to start. It would mean less work, cute light-blue uniforms, plenty of wealthy pilots, well-paid airline mechanics, and a base in Miami! *Airline passes will allow me to explore the world for cheap or for free! I love Miami and the beaches! Cuban coffee! Hot Latin lovers! No snow!*

I also love to travel and meet successful people! It's a no-brainer!

About the Author

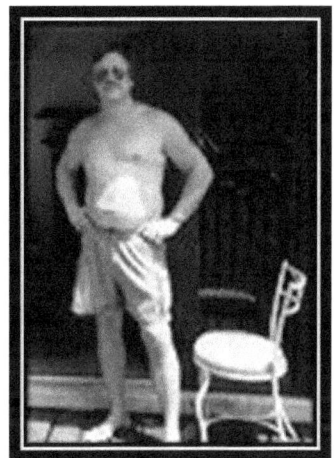

Beau Johnson lived in a Miami suburb for over fifty years and worked in Mental Health throughout South Florida for over twenty of those years. Retiring in 2007 he moved to Palm Coast, Florida, deciding to become a writer in that same year. Liberating Rhonda is a coming-of-age tale set in the sixties in The Midwest. It's the first part of an Adult Fiction trilogy he is writing about, loosely based on an old girlfriend in Miami he knew during that time. The sixties were a time of Civil Right marches and demonstrations, Women's' Liberation, expanding boundaries and sexual mores and freedoms.

His first short story published is Bob ad Marie, an end-of-life love story about Alzheimer's Disease and its effects on caregivers. He writes in self-defense, to keep his brain active and sharp.